The Dacha Husband

NORTHWESTERN WORLD CLASSICS

Northwestern World Classics brings readers
the world's greatest literature. The series features
essential new editions of well-known works,
lesser-known books that merit reconsideration,
and lost classics of fiction, drama, and poetry.
Insightful commentary and compelling new translations
help readers discover the joy of outstanding writing
from all regions of the world.

Ivan Shcheglov

The Dacha Husband

*His Adventures, Observations,
and Disappointments*

Translated from the Russian and with an
introduction by Michael R. Katz

Northwestern University Press ✦ *Evanston, Illinois*

Northwestern University Press
www.nupress.northwestern.edu

Printed in the United States of America

10 9 8 7 6 5 4 3 2 1

Library of Congress Cataloging-in-Publication Data
Shcheglov, Ivan, 1856–1911.
[Dachnyi muzh. English]
The dacha husband : his adventures, observations, and disappointments / Ivan Shcheglov ; translated from the Russian and with an introduction by Michael R. Katz.
p. cm. — (Northwestern world classics)
Includes bibliographical references.
ISBN 978-0-8101-2635-0 (pbk. : alk. paper)
I. Katz, Michael R. II. Title. III. Series: Northwestern world classics.
PG3467.L39D313 2009
891.733—dc22

2009023492

CONTENTS

Dacha is one of a very few Russian words that have entered common English usage (along with *tsar, samovar, Sputnik,* and *intelligentsia*—to cite the most familiar). A dacha is a country house or cottage used especially during the summer months. It is usually located close to a large urban center, since many heads of households continue to work through the summer months and commute into the city during the workweek, spending only weekends in the country.

The word *dacha* originally designated a "parcel of land granted by the prince."[1] It was derived from the common verb *dat'* (to give), and that, in turn, from the Indo-European root **dō-*. As a social and cultural institution, the Russian dacha has a long history that runs roughly parallel to the course of urbanization. The British historian Stephen Lovell has described this evolution at length in the informative monograph *Summerfolk: A History of the Dacha, 1710–2000.*[2]

Many well-known works of nineteenth-century Russian literature feature the dacha in some form as a setting of the action, beginning with Pushkin's tantalizing fragment of 1828, "The Guests Were Assembling at the Dacha," a piece that attracted Leo Tolstoy's admiration and attention as he was setting to work on his novel of adultery, *Anna Karenina;* Ivan Goncharov's classic *Oblomov* (1859); Ivan Turgenev's early tale "First Love" (1860); Fyodor Dostoevsky's second major novel, *The Idiot* (1868); and Anton Chekhov's final and most famous play, *The Cherry Orchard* (1904), in which Lopakhin's purchase of Madame Ranevskaya's estate—and his plan to chop down all the cherry trees, subdivide the land, and build dachas—symbolizes the economic and social decline of the Russian aristocracy.

✦

In 1708 Peter the Great presented a large estate outside the capital to his wife, Catherine I; but it was Peter's determined successor, Catherine II (the Great), who started to develop the place as a summer royal residence. By the end of the eighteenth century, Tsarskoye Selo (literally, "Tsar's Village") had become a popular site of summer habitation among Russian nobles eager to spend time residing near their sovereign. Fortunately, the town managed to escape the defacing impact of industrialization in the nineteenth century and was able to maintain its classical charm.

The adjacent village of Pavlovsk, located just south of Tsarskoye Selo, developed around the palace built by Catherine's son Paul I. When he ascended the Russian throne in 1796, the settlement surrounding his summer palace was large enough to be incorporated as a city. Prior to the 1917 revolution, Pavlovsk too had become a favorite summer retreat for well-to-do inhabitants of the capital.

The popularity of dachas near St. Petersburg was vastly increased by the development of rail transportation. The first year-round railway in Russia led from the capital to Tsarskoye Selo (fourteen miles), and from there on to Pavlovsk (sixteen miles). It was designed by the Viennese professor Franz Anton Von Gerstner, who had also built the first public railway on the European continent. In Russia he was commissioned to build only this short experimental line to demonstrate the feasibility of rail transportation in particular and, given the Russian climate, the possibility of operating locomotives during the winter months. Work on the single-track line was begun in 1835; the railway opened officially on October 30, 1837, when an eight-car train reached Tsarskoye Selo in an astonishing twenty-eight minutes. The extension to Pavlovsk was opened the following summer.[3]

From the beginning, Russian railway stations were constructed in what was thought to be the European style. At Pavlovsk, which soon became an increasingly popular destination for day trips from the capital, buffets and a ballroom were added to the building. The so-called Vauxhall Pavilion in Pavlovsk soon became the center of musical life for residents from St. Petersburg during the summer season.[4]

In general the Russian dacha was the primary summer dwelling place for women and children. Men continued to work in the city and to commute, while their wives and children enjoyed a life of relative leisure in the country. It is estimated that by 1891 some five thousand men were traveling to work daily in Petersburg. The image of the "dacha husband" was soon to become a cultural cliché. One late-nineteenth-century Russian dictionary of popular phrases describes this emerging phenomenon as

> a husband who leaves for work from the dacha and is commissioned to carry out various errands by his wife, sisters-in-law, mother-in-law, and neighbors.[5]

In its entry on *dacha,* the definitive seventeen-volume *Soviet Academy of Sciences Dictionary* defines *dachnyi muzh* as "the head of a family burdened by the need to transport supplies from town to the dacha."[6] The phrase first came into common usage only *after* the publication of Ivan Shcheglov's humorous novel *Dachnyi muzh* (*The Dacha Husband*) in 1888.

◆

Shcheglov was the pen name of Ivan Leontievich Leontiev (1856–1911), the grandson of a distinguished army general. He graduated from the Pavlovsk Military Academy and served in the artillery during the Caucasian War (1877–78). He retired from the army with the rank of captain. In 1881 he attracted considerable attention with his tale of military life, "The First Battle." Other short stories appeared in various periodicals and earned him a reputation as one of Russia's most promising young writers.

After the enormous success of *The Dacha Husband,* Shcheglov wrote several works attacking the followers of Leo Tolstoy, the so-called Tolstoyans, both their intentions and their activities. By so doing, he forfeited the sympathy of many of his early admirers. From the 1890s onward he specialized in writing humorous stories and plays, mostly of a lighthearted and diverting nature, lacking both cutting satire and serious themes. During his lifetime Shcheglov's plays were produced regularly and have now become a permanent part of the repertoire of amateur theater groups.

The book that is arguably Shcheglov's best work is his novel *The Dacha Husband.* It provides a remarkably realistic and highly entertaining account of the emerging Russian middle class at the end of the nineteenth century. It introduces a new character type in Russian literature, the "dacha husband" (*dachnyi muzh*), which deserves to take its place alongside the "superfluous man" (*lishnii chelovek*) in the pantheon of classic character types. The subtitle of Shcheglov's novel foreshadows the plot: *His Adventures, Observations, and Disappointments.* The work became extremely popular, and the author took advantage of its fame by recasting it in dramatic form. The play was frequently performed on the St. Petersburg stage to the great delight of its audiences.

In addition to the portrait of the emerging middle class, Shcheglov's novel made a significant contribution to the so-called woman question (*zhenskii vopros*) in Russian culture. This phrase was used in connection with major social changes taking place in the second half of the nineteenth century that led to a reexamination of the fundamental roles of women in society.

For Russian readers, it was particularly the writings of George Sand (1804–76), pseudonym of Amandine Aurore Lucile Dudevant (née Dupin), whose life and works exerted the greatest influence on culture and behavior. It will be recalled that George Sand left her husband and family in the French countryside in 1831 and returned to Paris to take up literature, in addition to becoming the mistress of several writers, artists, philosophers, musicians, and politicians. She wrote over one hundred books, including autobiographical accounts of her notorious affairs with the poet Alfred de Musset and the composer Frédéric Chopin. Sand's description of the passions of the heart, and in particular, her insistence on the theme of freedom in love, found a warm welcome among the predominantly female readers of the Russian capital.

Beginning in 1836 George Sand's novels flooded Russia, first in French and then in translation.[7] The eternal and seemingly insoluble problem of the "love triangle," first treated in her novel *Jacques* (1848), next imitated by Russian writers, was then transformed into the basis of several important nineteenth-century Russian novels: Alexander Herzen's *Who Is to Blame?* (1846), Alexander Druzhinin's *Polinka Saks* (1847), and Nikolai Chernyshevsky's *What Is to Be Done?* (1863).[8] Each of these novels, though inspired by Sand, proposed a different and original resolution to the dilemma of the romantic triangle.

But, as we know, actions speak louder than words: according to several well-documented sources, some Russian women began to adopt the behavior of Sand's uninhibited heroines as their model. In the name of "free love," "true feeling," and "individual choice," passionate Russian ladies fell for seducers and conquerors, suave European lovers, and dashing Caucasian horsemen. This was the cultural background against which Shcheglov's novel should be read and enjoyed.

One important fashion note: the hero of the novel describes at some length the pernicious impact of one particular aspect of women's clothing—to wit, the *tournure* or bustle,[9] a type of frame used to expand the fullness or support the drapery at the back of a woman's dress. It was worn underneath the skirt, fastened just below the waist, and—together with a corset—managed to accentuate the woman's rump, waist, and bust. At the time the effect was perceived as a highly erotic, even provocative, declaration of female sexuality. In Shcheglov's mildly misogynistic novel, the bustle became a powerful symbol of woman's infidelity, perfidy, treachery, and other assorted faults.

When *Dachnyi muzh* was published in 1888, the author sent a copy to Chekhov with the inscription "To my dear, sweet Egmont—to remember the ill-fated Alba."[10] The reference, of course, was to Goethe's Shakespearean drama *Egmont* (1788). The brave Flemish warrior Egmont wages a futile struggle for independence against the despotic Spanish invader Alba and dies a martyr to the cause of justice and national liberty. Shcheglov is here acknowledging Chekhov's clear superiority as a man of letters.[11]

Leontiev's pen name, Shcheglov, also hints at his modest estimation of his own literary talents. Derived from the word *shchegol* (goldfinch), it was borrowed from a well-known animal fable entitled "The Starling," by Ivan Krylov (1768–1844), which concludes as follows:

> Better to sing well like a goldfinch,
> Than badly like a nightingale.[12]

So Leontiev, even in his choice of a pen name, recognizes that he himself has come to be satisfied with his own singing like a twittering goldfinch, rather than compete with a writer such as Chekhov, who, of course, sang like a mellifluous nightingale.

Yet Chekhov continued to consider Shcheglov as one of the most promising young authors of the decade. In a letter written in 1888 he states: "People are talking a lot about Shcheglov, who in my opinion is [both] talented and original."[13] The two writers collaborated on an amusing farce entitled *The Power of Hypnotism*.[14] They also kept up a playful correspondence; their frequent letters are packed with private jokes and teasing references. In one particularly appreciative letter dated February 22, 1888, Chekhov wrote to Shcheglov:

> I read through all your books, which up to now I had
> read only in fits and starts. If you want some criticism,
> here it is. First of all, it seems to me that you cannot be
> compared with Gogol, Tolstoy, or Dostoevsky, as all your
> reviewers seem to do. You are a writer *sui generis* and as
> independent as an eagle in the sky. . . . In general, one
> must be careful with comparisons that, innocent though
> they may be, always unintentionally arouse suspicions
> and accusations of imitation and deception. For heaven's
> sake, don't believe your colleagues; continue working just
> as you have been. Your language, style, and characters, as
> well as your long descriptions and pithy depictions—all
> this is your own, it's original, and very good indeed.[15]

✦

This is the first English translation of Shcheglov's *Dacha Husband* and is being offered in the hope that its readers will find it both *dulce et utile,* "sweet and useful," entertaining and informative. Chekhov was right on the mark: Shcheglov's "language, style, and characters" are absolutely "original" and *very,* "very good indeed."

I have chosen to translate the second, slightly expanded edition, *Dachnyi muzh: ego pokhozhdeniya, nablyudeniya i razocharovaniya, Vtoroe dopolnennoe izdanie.* (St. Petersburg: Izd. M.M. Lederle, 1896.)

I would like to acknowledge Professor Lawrence Senelick (Tufts University), whose article in the *Bulletin of the North American Chekhov Society* (Autumn 2005) first sparked my interest in Shcheglov's novel and whose kind words encouraged me to undertake this endeavor. I am also grateful to Professor Stephen Lovell (King's College, London) for his comprehensive history of the Russian dacha and his enthusiasm for my project. I owe a special debt of gratitude to Lecturer Emerita Alexandra Baker (Middlebury College) for her careful reading of my draft and the many helpful suggestions she made. Finally, the two anonymous readers for Northwestern University Press provided excellent corrections and suggestions from which I have benefited enormously. My sincere thanks go to all of the above.

Michael R. Katz
Middlebury College

Notes

1. M. Fasmer, *Etimologicheskii slovar' russkogo yazyka*. Moscow: Progress, 1964, I, 485–86.

2. Stephen Lovell, Ithaca, N.Y.: Cornell University Press, 2003.

3. J. N. Westwood, *A History of Russian Railways*. London: Allen and Unwin, 1964, 21–25.

4. The Russian word for "station," *vokzal,* is most likely derived from the English word *Vauxhall.*

5. M. I. Mikhel'son, *Russkaya mysl' i rech': Opyt russkoi frazeologii*. St. Petersburg: Akademiya nauk, 1899, 27. Quoted in Lovell, 99.

6. *Slovar' sovremennogo russkogo literaturnogo yazyka*. Moscow-Leningrad: Academy of Sciences, 1954, III, 565–66.

7. See Richard Stites, *The Women's Liberation Movement in Russia: Feminism, Nihilism, and Bolshevism, 1860–1920*. Princeton: Princeton University Press, 1978, 19–23.

8. My own translations of these three novels are available: Herzen's *Who Is to Blame?* was published by Cornell University Press in 1984; Druzhinin's *Polinka Saks* by Northwestern University Press in 1992; and Chernyshevsky's *What Is to Be Done?* by Cornell University Press in 1989.

9. The Russian word *turnyur* is clearly a borrowing from the French *tournure,* from the Latin meaning "to turn." While British English uses either *tournure* or *bustle,* American usage seems limited to the latter, which I use in this translation.

10. A. P. Chekhov, *Polnoe sobranie sochinenii i pisem.* Moscow: Nauka, 1975, *Pis'ma,* v. 2, 436.

11. This parallels Vasily Zhukovsky's famous inscription on the small portrait of himself he sent to Alexander Pushkin on the occasion of the publication of the latter's first successful narrative poem, *Ruslan and Lyudmila* (1821): "To the victorious pupil from his vanquished mentor."

12. Donald Rayfield, *Anton Chekhov: A Life.* New York: Holt Publishers, 1997, 161.

13. *Anton Chekhov's Life and Thought: Selected Letters and Commentary,* translated by Michael Heim in collaboration with Simon Karlinsky. Berkeley: University of California Press, 1975, 93.

14. Translated and published in a new collection, *The Complete Plays of Anton Chekhov,* by Lawrence Senelick. New York: Norton Publishers, 2006.

15. Chekhov, *Pis'ma,* v. 2, 204. My translation.

Vous l'avez voulu. George Dandin, vous l'avez voulu!
Molière

The Dacha Husband first announced its existence ten years ago in the pages of the journal *New Time*—thus, the present edition, coinciding with its "tenth anniversary," is, so to speak, a "jubilee" edition! It would be useless to conceal the fact that at such a time my heart is overflowing with authorial pride. As is well known, man is always inclined to be proud of something: one person takes pride in having identified a new ballet star; a second, in having invented a new compound for removing stains from trousers; a third, in having discovered a new microbe in the human organism. As for me, I take pride in the fact that I identified . . . the "dacha husband"! I'm also proud that this modest but instructive discovery engendered an enviable quantity of imitations, beginning with Anton Chekhov's famous parody-vaudeville *An Unwilling Tragedian* and ending with the comedy-vaudeville[1] *The Dacha Husband* belonging to my close colleague and fellow writer . . . Ivan Shcheglov-the-dramatist. But, alas, there is one circumstance clouding the celebratory condition of my spirit: I confess that I'm troubled by the rapid success of civilization in the last ten years that has so altered the condition of the dacha husband with the result that some details of the book may seem out of date for readers at the end of the current century.

My goodness, how quickly we advance! Just think of all the things that have been invented lately for the comfort of humankind: Brown-Sekarovsky elixir[2] for bolstering the low spirits and bodies of dacha husbands; a family bicycle built for three so that the dacha husband, dacha wife, and dacha cousin can all ride together; and—last but not least—Professor Roentgen's diabolical apparatus that allows one to ascertain well in advance whether or not a heart lies beneath the corset of one's beloved![3]

Will all these inventions enhance or damage the situation of the dacha husband? Time, of course, will tell—but, in the meantime, it falls to me, as a writer who describes everyday life, to clarify this equivocal matter.

In justified expectation of a grateful response from those dacha husbands living in Petersburg, I have the honor of being their obedient servant,

Ivan Shcheglov
St. Petersburg
April 1, 1896

Notes

Epigraph: "You wanted it, George Dandin, you wanted it!" *George Dandin ou le Mari confondu* (*The Confused Husband*) is a comedy by Molière written in 1668. It showcases the folly of a man who marries a woman of higher rank and has to endure the extravagant whims and fancies of his headstrong wife.

1. These two terms, *parody-vaudeville* and *comedy-vaudeville,* are coined by the author. They are not generally used in literary criticism.

2. This elixir was a popular remedy used for various ailments.

3. Wilhelm Roentgen (1845–1923) was the German physicist who first detected and produced X-rays in 1895.

The Dacha Husband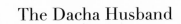

1

What Is a Dacha Husband?

DO YOU KNOW, LADIES AND GENTLEMEN, what a "dacha husband" is? You don't? Let me say that you're being devious. However, it's the worse for you since now I intend to explain fully the fatal meaning of this phrase. It's very easy for me to do since for the last three years I've been renting a dacha for my wife in Pavlovsk* and making the trip to work in Petersburg every day, and every day cursing the day I was born. You're smiling and you're at a loss; you're ready to agree with my wife that I'm a grouch and a misanthrope, or you simply think that I didn't sleep well last night and am being difficult. Well, as a matter of fact, I didn't get enough sleep last night, and the same goes for the night before, and the night before that, too . . . and I shall never get enough sleep as long as this accursed nomadic-dacha situation continues. Judge for yourselves. Yesterday my wife and I came home after 10:00 P.M. with the Golokhvastov family from a musical evening, and after drinking some tea, we kept playing "a bit of vint"† until well past 2:00 A.M. Needless to say, I fell into bed like a corpse in the hope of getting some sleep. But that was not to be. At eight o'clock in the morning, "at the most interesting moment," just as I was dreaming that I'd won two hundred thousand rubles

---

*A town located near Petersburg that developed around a splendid residence of the Russian imperial family. It soon became a favorite summer resort for well-to-do inhabitants of the capital.

†Vint is a Russian card game, similar to both bridge and whist.

and had tendered my resignation, someone shouted into my ear: "Ivan Grigorevich, wake up! Ivan Grigorevich, you're going to be late for the train again. The mistress will be very angry!" I rub my eyes and before me I see the face of Stepan, and behind his lackey back—the entire distressing reality of my situation: alas, not only did I not win two hundred thousand rubles, but yesterday I lost my shirt in vint, and a huge amount of work has accumulated in the department due to my director's departure to take the waters; in addition, I have less than half an hour to wash, dress, drink some tea, and race to the station . . .* I get dressed in a hurry; choking and burning my mouth, I manage to down a glass of tea; I shove my briefcase under my arm, and, like a madman, race to the train. . . . I'm not far from the station when I hear the second bell. What's to be done? I forget the fact that I'm a state councilor and, hugging my briefcase tight against my chest, I start skipping like a schoolboy; panting and swearing, I reach the platform. I barely manage to buy a ticket when the third bell deafens me. . . . A few more steps at a gallop and—at last I reach the train car. . . . Oof! The train pulls away. . . .

"Isn't it a fine morning?" Peter Ivanovich says, addressing me. He's also a dacha husband, who happens to be sitting just opposite.

"En . . . en . . . enchanting!" I mumble, wiping large drops of sweat from my face and apologizing with my eyes for not having noticed dear Peter Ivanovich.

Isn't it true, ladies and gentlemen, what a pleasant morning it is?

But it's still not all that bad. At least my wife didn't accompany me to the station, and that's already a great relief.

On the ill-starred day when she takes it into her head to escort me to the station and accomplishes the feat of getting up

*The very first railway in Russia was opened between St. Petersburg and Pavlovsk in 1837.

early—I'm awakened by the cock's crowing. My wife requires a good two hours to dress, fix her hair, and to impart to her face the freshness of morning color. At last, she's ready. She's sporting her brilliantly conceived, elegantly flirtatious, and, at the same time, informally simple attire that bears witness to the fact she manages to "follow" simultaneously her husband, as well as the latest Parisian fashions. Naturally, we reach the platform together; I get a ticket, and then a touching scene ensues: my wife takes me on a survey of all the cars and searches for a place where I will be the most comfortable (?). At last, the "best place" is located, the first bell sounds, and I take my seat. Having fulfilled, in her own opinion, all the responsibilities required of an exemplary wife, she pauses next to my window and smugly glances at the passing dacha husbands with their equally exemplary wives. There follows the usual question: "Jean, will you be home for dinner?"

"Of course, I will."

"On the four o'clock train?"

"Ah, my dear, as if you didn't know!"

"Mind you don't linger in town. Or else the soup will get cold again; then you'll fall asleep after dinner and we'll be late for the concert!"

Pause. My wife fixes her hair and for a while stares thoughtfully at the cloudless sky, obviously demonstrating that love for her husband involuntarily awakens in her a love of nature.

"Ah, Jean, I almost forgot!" she says to me, innocently and merrily raising her made-up eyes. "My dress is ready to be picked up from Mlle Tyurlyurlyu. . . . Do you remember, you promised to fetch it?"

"Is that Mlle Tyurlyurlyu on Morskaya Street?" I ask in a faint voice, oppressed by the foreboding of imminent assignments.

"Yes, on Morskaya, my dear, in the same building where the Spitsins live. Yes . . . and one more thing." (My wife's face suddenly assumes a serious, businesslike expression.) "For heaven's sake, don't forget to drop by Kochkurov's to pick up the sweets. With your absentmindedness, you've probably managed to forget that tonight, after the concert, we've invited Nadezhda Romanovna and her daughter over to tea?"

"No, dear, I haven't forgotten," I say with a sigh.

Ding, ding, ding! Thank heavens, the second bell. At this moment at the far end of the platform there appears a cherubic young man in yellow clodhoppers, a blue morning coat, and some sort of ridiculous hat. It's my wife's newly discovered cousin—Sergei Mikhailovich Bolonkin. She immediately becomes more animated.

"Good morning, Sergei Mikhailovich!" she says, greeting Bolonkin. "How nice that you've come. You'll escort me home, won't you? Isn't it just along your way?"

"Why, yes, of course it is!" Bolonkin says with a smile, gallantly bowing and scraping (for these despicable "cousins," it's always just along their way with other men's wives!).

"Jean, this is Sergei Mikhailovich!"

We exchange a cool handshake. But my selfless labor has not yet ended. My wife's face unexpectedly assumes a genuinely apprehensive look and she begins to search nervously in her wicker handbag.

"Now, wouldn't it be splendid if I didn't find it?" she says with a smile, pulling from her handbag some sort of lace remnant and casting a coquettishly imploring glance at me: "My dear, here's what else I want to ask you: when you go past the shopping arcade, call in at 8 Perinnaya Lane just for a moment. Buy nine and a half arshins* of this kind of lace insertion. . . ." She gives me the sample. "Please, don't forget. It's very important to me!"

I obediently stash the piece in my pocket, but, alas, after the "lace insertion," there come "gloves with six buttons" and a

*A Russian unit of measurement equivalent to twenty-eight inches.

request to "keep an eye out" in the office for a new wet nurse, since the current one is pining for her husband and demanding a raise.

"However, I don't want to burden you, my dear," my wife adds condescendingly, "if you don't have time to check on the wet nurse, at least get the gloves!" And she assumes an elegantly meek pose that says without a word: "Aren't I an angel?" I don't know what might've come after the wet nurse and the gloves if, at long last, the benefactor and savior of all dacha husbands hadn't appeared on the platform—the stationmaster. . . .

Hurrah! The third bell, a whistle, and the train starts to move. . . .

"Good-bye, Jean, don't forget what I've asked you!"

"I'll try, *ma chère.** Good-bye!"

The train pulls away and I watch from the window as my wife goes off arm in arm with Monsieur Bolonkin.

I find this Pavlovsk cousin of ours definitely suspicious! He doesn't drink vodka, doesn't play cards, and he's constantly plying my wife with French novels. I'm afraid that he'll get her so used to reading during the summer that I won't be able to break her of the habit all winter long!

As of late so many of these pernicious cousins have turned up at the dachas—it's simply impossible! Why doesn't the government do something about it? They take steps against the gophers that devour the grain. . . . It's true that we contemporary husbands are not in the best position!

As depressing as all this is, I still didn't get enough sleep, and therefore, abandoning this useless philosophizing, I hasten to make up along the way for time not slept.

And here I am in Petersburg. . . . "Driver, to the corner of such and such street!" The driver takes me to that corner and, a quarter of an hour later, I reach the goal of my journey—the

*My dear (Fr.). French titles and phrases were conventionally used by Russians of a certain class.

department offices. During the supervisor's "vacation," I carry out his duties, and consequently all the office work falls on my shoulders. . . . Immense quantities of paper have accumulated, and toil as we might, the quantity not only doesn't diminish, but somehow even manages to increase. The stuffiness in the office is unbearable, and with each passing hour I feel more dim-witted. . . . By four o'clock—the time work ends—I've already lost the ability to think. . . . And now it's necessary to carry out all my wife's commissions before catching the train home. . . . Naturally I'm late for it and, as a result, late for dinner. The heat's intolerable. There's literally nothing to breathe in the train car. It's also absolutely impossible to read, because in the summer edition of the newspaper one finds only the same void that exists in one's own head. . . . Only one recourse remains: to suffer and endure, just as everyone else suffers and endures in a train filled with all these dacha husbands, closely resembling a car of arrested criminals. At last we reach Pavlovsk! Covered with dust, exhausted, hungry, and staggering under the weight of boxes from Mlle Tyurlyurlyu, I finally arrive at the dacha. While passing through the room leading to the balcony, I notice the pernicious cousin's ridiculous hat on the piano, and next to it, a reprehensible little yellowish volume with the fatal title *Crime d'amour.* . . .[*] But when a man's hungry as a wolf, naturally he has no time for jealousy. I come upon a touching trio on the balcony: my wife, her cousin, and our pug, Othello. On the table are the dramatic traces of the dinner consumed. My wife's first words were, "Jean, haven't you eaten?" In reply to the ominous growling of my stomach, she says with a playfully grief-stricken smile: "Sergei Mikhailovich and I have just finished the pastries. As a punishment for your being so late, we've left you no dessert!" Thanks to this dacha gopher, I missed dessert almost all summer! "You're at fault: I

[*]*A Crime of Love* (Fr.).

came to meet your train both at four and at five o'clock! It's a good thing Sergei Mikhailovich was kind enough to escort me home and agreed to share a bowl of soup with me."

I smile artificially and, now like a wolf, apply myself to the cool soup, the leftovers of calves' feet, and the skeleton of what must have been a very tasty fish.

After dinner I don't have long to think; without ceremony I sprawl out on the divan, while my wife sets off with our cousin to water the flowers in the garden. I let them busy themselves with natural history for as long as they like, dreaming of only one thing—catching up on my sleep. But my dream is to remain just that, a dream: in less than an hour they come to wake me rudely. Before me stands my wife in an indignant pose, ready to leave for the concert, in all the incomprehensible madness of her newly invented toilet.

"Ivan Grigorevich, you're simply becoming unbearable! You neglect absolutely everything on earth for your divan! You've probably even forgotten that you live in Pavlovsk, that you have a wife, and that today's the benefit concert for Glavach!" Having learned from long experience, I consider it superfluous to justify myself, and I hurry to dress. The reigning moral code at the dacha is as follows: a wife who spends the morning strolling arm in arm with her cousin and the evening with her husband is commendable; a wife who does just the opposite is beyond compare. Yielding to this seasonal morality, I obediently stick to my unnatural side of the bargain, and we set off for the station.

At the concert, needless to say, it's all the same: the very same Glavach is on stage; the same acquaintances are annoyed by the "public" for whom they've come, the ones who listen to music with as much attention as they do to the buzzing of a tiresome mosquito; the same senseless, deadening, and for some reason, appealing "rush to lunge" ahead following the same vicious circle around the benches, where, once a person starts, he's involuntarily transformed into some kind of mechanically moving marionette. So I too move back and forth around this vicious circle, inhaling the abundant dust and the smell of the bustling grove; I keep moving, and at the same time I muse about the fate of a contemporary man of culture. . . . It's strange, I think, how the life of contemporary man has taken shape! Can it really be that all the great suffering of our upbringing, all one's intellectual efforts in pursuit of a career, and then all the anxiety of the nervous system expended in order to maintain one's position, that all this leads, in the last analysis, to one thing only—this treacherous, enchanted circle?

"Jean, why aren't you clapping for Glavach? He's played his piece," my wife asks, yanking my sleeve. I gloomily applaud Glavach for his composition and my day at the dacha ends in the usual way: late tea, playing vint until 2:00 A.M. at our place or at the kind neighbors', followed by the usual lack of sleep and the usual morning hellish gallop with my briefcase under my arm from our dacha to the train platform.

Oh, Lord, for what sins do you punish contemporary man so cruelly?

You're laughing again? You think I'm seeing things too dismally? Oh, I know well in advance what objection you'll make: "What about Sunday? Let's assume that everything you've said is the absolute truth; you still have Sunday, a blessed day of rest for all those who toil!"

Come, come, ladies and gentlemen! Don't you know what Sunday in Pavlovsk is really like for a genuine dacha husband who lives in the center of town and whose dacha faces the street? Take yesterday for example. I intentionally got up early and settled down in the gazebo with a newspaper, a cigar, and a cup of coffee. It was a beautiful morning. There were all sorts of subtle aromas in the air, butterflies fluttering, birds singing, and so on. . . . I was almost ready to believe in the poetry of life at the dacha. But the illusion didn't last long. A quarter of an hour hadn't passed when right in front of our balcony, appearing as if from nowhere, arose monster number one, and, fixing his eyes on me, he bawled out in a falsetto voice: "Kerchiefs, linens, Russian towels!" No doubt he thought that I'd come from town without linens and that I had nothing to use to wipe my face. I'd hardly managed to send this first tormentor to the devil when two more popped up from behind his back. One shouted at the top of his lungs: "Combs, pomade!" and the other cried in an excruciating voice, "Shoes, low boots!" It occurred to neither of these two scoundrels that my hair was already combed and that I was already wearing shoes. I lowered the curtain and cover myself with the newspaper. But this didn't help one bit. These virtuosos possess a dog's nose and can sniff out a summer resident through a stone wall. And sure enough, every five minutes or so, my ears were assaulted by the most absurd propositions: one offers Russian lace, another, Dutch herrings, a third, beads, a fourth, walnuts, a fifth, to sharpen my knives, a sixth, to inhale lilies of the valley, a seventh, to purchase ink and paper, an eighth, to buy Swedish bread, a ninth, Swedish matches, a tenth, wild game, the eleventh, twelfth, and thirteenth, fresh fish, children's toys, and even oleographs. . . .* Ugh! And is that everything? What about the Petersburg Italians, voicing their longing for their homeland, various Punch-and-Judy shows, Hungarian violinists, German trumpeters, and the rest of the musical rascals? Well, I have to admit—it's the dacha! The devil only knows whether it's coated in honey—perhaps that's why it attracts so many of these pests!

But then my "personal enemy" appeared on the stage, acting out his role in front of my window several times a day with beastly persistence: "Fine chocolate, good candy, lemonade,

---

*An oleograph is a chromolithograph printed on cloth to imitate an oil painting.

tasty spice cakes!" he barked, at first from the middle of the street, then repeating his aria moving over on the right side, then again, on the left—suddenly, completely unexpectedly, coming right up to the glass of the gallery, he screeched, "An old friend has arrived!" Oh, damn it all! I jumped up as if I'd been stung, headed for the very back of the balcony, and sat with my back facing the street. At that very moment the door to the balcony opened and my wife appeared on the threshold, dressed to the nines. Seeing me in my dressing gown and slippers, at first she was too appalled to say anything. Unfortunately, her speech returned, and she let loose a stream of invectives: "Ivan Grigorevich, have you completely lost your mind? It's almost one o'clock, do you hear, you unfortunate man, it's almost one o'clock in the afternoon! Did you really forget that the Nenyukovs and their children from Tsarskoye Selo* are planning to visit us today and spend the afternoon here? Yes, indeed—you forgot! Tell me, where's your memory? Did you leave it in town? If only you could spare me! They could be here any minute, and you're still wearing God knows what!"

Then the bell.

My wife hurried to thrust her head out the open window of the balcony facing the street. Damnation—it *was* the Nenyukovs! With lightning speed Marya Dmitrievna cast a glance at me and disappeared into the living room. Seeing that any escape through the public rooms was cut off, I covered my face with the newspaper, and hitching up the hem of my dressing gown, I ran like a madman through the garden, the courtyard, and the kitchen to my room upstairs to change my clothes. . . .

Ladies and gentlemen, in your opinion, is this life, or perhaps even "paradise"? Do you consider the existence of a dacha husband completely normal?

I thank you kindly.

---

*The former residence of the Russian imperial family near St. Petersburg; it became a popular place of summer residence among the nobility.

2

Little Babylon

MORNING IN PAVLOVSK. . . . A beautiful July morning. The sun has long since risen and is shining its cheerful light on backyards and front gardens of the finest dachas. Waves of fragrance waft from balconies covered in flowers. . . . Bees buzz, flirtatiously arrayed butterflies flutter, and sparrows and swallows clustered under the roof chirp loudly and provocatively, as if unable to understand how it's possible to sleep until nine o'clock on such a splendid morning. But the day at the dacha has not yet begun, and the curtains on the windows and balconies are still drawn; streets and boulevards are cheerless and deserted. From time to time a dacha husband—late for the train, with circles under his eyes, a sleepy face, and a briefcase under his arm—rushes along the boulevard; a schoolboy in a light linen uniform with a towel around his shoulders, an inveterate devotee of swimming, fishing, and boating, runs past; or else Vanya the yardman, in going to fetch some water, stops at the crossroads to exchange pleasantries with Marya the maid hastening to the bakery, and she agrees to a rendezvous "beyond the river in the dead of night. . . ." Then everything becomes cheerless and deserted once again.

From 9:30 to 11:30 A.M. occurs the deluge of various dacha troubadours touting their "wild game," "crisp greens," "fresh salmon," and so forth.* The cries of these troubadours cause

*Nikolai Gogol's short story "Nevsky Prospect" (1835) presents a comparable description of a day in the life of the fashionable capital.

the curtains of some balconies to open, and behind the curtains some sleepy peignoirs appear; these sleepy peignoirs wave to the "wild game" and the "fresh salmon," inviting them into the courtyard, and then they hide. All this is, so to speak, the dacha overture. The actual day at the dacha begins around 1:00 P.M. By this time elegant "bustling caravans" appear on the streets and boulevards. Glistening in the sunlight and displaying all their splendor, they slowly stretch from all sides and in all directions, gradually gathering at their bustling center—the station.*

If you want to know where the world is heading, stand somewhere near the gate and look very carefully. Pay attention, for example, to this little group—a mama and a wet nurse, pushing a year-old cherub in a carriage. There's no reason to glance into the carriage: under the pile of muslin and white silk lace, you can scarcely make out a pink button of a nose; on the other hand, if you glance even fleetingly at the mother and wet nurse, you'll see immediately what philosophers search for in vain—the truth about women. Look at the wet nurse, a Russian wet nurse, wearing a fine peasant headdress and a blue tunic, loosely outlining her strong shape. A tall, fair-skinned beauty with an open rosy face and an ample bosom, she's blooming with good health and the joy of life. . . . Now look at the mother, at the small, pale, nervously flirtatious contemporary mother. You can hardly see her: there, where a woman's head is supposed to be—only her chin and the back of her head are visible; everything else is covered by some monstrous crimson saddle of a hat; and there, where her bosom, waist, and so on are supposed to be, so many expensive rags and scraps of cloth are tossed and twisted, that your eyes are at a loss to discern where things begin and where they end. . . . I bet that while glancing at the former, the thought occurs to you:

*The station building was also used as a concert hall.

"There's a woman as created by the Lord God!" And, glancing at the latter, you think: "There's a woman redesigned according to fashion by the devil!"

Or else, admire these two pallid young ladies, strutting pretentiously in the company of their stuffy governess in the blue pince-nez with a copy of *The Cordial Word** under her arm. The girls appear to be no older than seven, but they're already meticulously enveloped in corsets and wearing boots with double heels; these two small affected girls wear fashionable "windmills" on their heads; on their hands, bracelets and gloves; and behind, an indispensable bustle, which, with childish vanity, they wiggle very sweetly and amusingly. And the boys, ill-fated Russian boys, how they dress them up! Looking like jockeys, clowns, Turks, almost Zulus, when there already exists a splendid, entirely salutary, inexpensive Russian attire; but today's mothers seem to have forgotten all about that, just as they forget everything on earth except that Pavlovsk is a center for bustles and that in the morning one must attend the "morning concert," and in the evening, the "evening concert."

From two to four in the afternoon the military orchestra plays in the small pavilion of the station. This is the so-called matinee concert for children—why it's for children is decidedly difficult to understand. In such a case one could produce with the same good reason "a matinee *La belle Hélène*† for children" in the Pavlovsk theater, since the orchestra, playing through the entire repertoire of operettas, the mother-Helens, all dressed to the nines, and, flirting with them, in the absence of the dacha-husband-Menelauses, the cousin-Parises, present a scene that is not edifying in the least. As a matter of fact this "morning concert" is simply a comedy—something like a secret preparatory school of female flirtation for girls no

*A popular children's journal, *Zadushevnoe slovo* (1877–1918).
†An opéra bouffe (1864) by the German-born French composer Jacques Offenbach (1819–80).

more than ten years old (older girls practice this art with considerable success at the evening concerts). The picture that emerges is rather instructive. The orchestra plays potpourris of "Gypsy songs." The nice mothers sit at little garden tables and admire how their sweet children—also dressed to the nines according to the latest fashion, holding hands—dance around the musicians' gazebo to the stirring sounds of the Tigryonek.* One would have to be blind not to see how these little girls, shown off so vaingloriously, do their utmost to compete with one another to appear more attractive and more flirtatious. Dressed like Zulus, the boys usually don't participate in the bustle dance and merely court the six- to eight-year-old "subjects" during intermission. The potpourris of Gypsy songs act as a progressive stimulus. Even the above-mentioned one-year-old piglet in white silk lace, dozing to the music in his carriage, breathes in curiously through his nostrils and tries to lift up his head and free it from the surrounding lace swaddling clothes.

> They say I'm a little dev-v-vil,
> Scarcely out of diap-p-pers!

The orchestra grinds on. . . . And the piglet in white silk lace happily falls asleep to the sound of this dacha lullaby.

And here's a scene of another kind: a strict mother sits at a table and reads the pornographic stories of Catulle Mendès;† between stories she's trying to educate her daughter, a pretty, fair-haired little one, dressed up like a Parisian doll and obviously bored by her solitude. The frisky child shakes her curls in annoyance and squints at the sky. From this movement her fashionable little feathered hat slides down the back of her head. Offense number one.

*Literally, "tiger cub" (Rus.); a fashionable dance.
†A prolific French poet, critic, and novelist of the Parnassian School (1841–1909).

"Adya, aren't you ashamed? Look at what you've done to your hat!"

Adya adjusts her hat and begins digging in the sand. Offense number two.

"Adya, *finessez tout de suite!*[*] You're soiling your lace!"

The irrepressible Adya, seeing that she can find consolation neither in the sky nor on the earth, begins singing something plaintive. The strict mama interrupts her reading and with some annoyance places Adya next to her.

"Today you're behaving like a crazy person. . . . It's time you understood that you live in Pavlovsk, not in the country!"

The ill-starred Adya, absolutely failing to understand why she lives in Pavlovsk and not in the country, apprehensively opens her eyes wide and sits absolutely still in her seat.

The poor, innocent little bustle!

Around 4:00 P.M. the children's concert ends, and the center of gravity at the dachas switches to the train platform. The mother-Helens let the cousin-Parises go in peace and, primly smartening themselves up, wait for their dacha-husband-Menelauses to arrive from town. This "ceremonial divorce" to some extent is a "bustle competition" in the prowess of their toilet among dacha wives, a curious arsenal of female envy, hypocrisy, and coquetry. . . . But now the signal bell sounds. Bustles sway nervously, hairdos are adjusted primly, and powdered faces assume a combined expression of conjugal ecstasy and "preprandial" indisposition. The steam engine, sighing philosophically, approaches the station and drags behind it a multicolored assortment of hot containers with heated meat pies . . . that is to say, dacha husbands. Worn out from the heat, breathing hard and wiping perspiration from their faces, the husbands approach their respective bustle-wearing sovereigns and report that the commissions entrusted to them have been

*Stop that at once (Fr.).

successfully completed. The dacha wives accept these reports graciously, take their pale slaves by the arm—and the spousal caravans journey home.

From 5:00 to 6:00 P.M. occurs the feeding of dacha husbands.

From six o'clock on there begins the so-called ice-cream period. After six each and every decent dacha resident considers it his absolute duty to stuff him or herself with crème brûlée or pistachio ice cream. Near some gates stand beckoning maids or footmen, whose duty it is to entice their favorite ice-cream vendors. In this regard, women's tastes are extremely fickle: one considers that the best ice cream can be had from the brunet who brings it on a white horse; another considers that, on the contrary, the blond who rides the chestnut mare is incomparably more obliging. About five years ago such whims did not exist, and only two stray ice-cream vendors made their way through the whole town on foot. At the present time however, an entire squadron of vendors has assembled, which, having divided Pavlovsk into "ice-cream districts," dispatches on foraging expeditions the most enticing ice-cream vendors on horseback. It's shocking to realize how much ice cream is consumed between the hours of 6:00 and 7:00 P.M.! Everyone eats ice cream—papas, mamas, young ladies, pupils, governesses, and children; lately even dogs have acquired this taste of dacha life. Please, don't take this as a joke: my wife's pug Othello is apportioned a precise amount of orange ice cream every day, which he consumes with the self-satisfied air of a well-brought-up dacha dog. After all this ice cream, it isn't surprising that the wives of Pavlovsk are significantly colder to their husbands than the wives of some place like Ligov or Siverskaya.[*]

From 7:30 to 8:30 P.M. there are new bustle-caravans heading in the direction of an evening concert, the summer theater,

---

[*]Ligov is a city in the Donetsk province of Ukraine; Siverskaya is located some fifty miles south of Petersburg.

or even "to the moon"—in a word, wherever it promises to be merrier, judging from the assorted announcements posted in abundance on trees and lampposts. With each passing year the spider of boredom spreads his web of entertainment farther and farther over the ill-starred dacha folks who fail to take pleasure in the bosom of nature. . . . And what don't these sheets promise? On one tree Mr. Glavach tempts you with a splendid concert "on a newly invented harmonium," Moscow Gypsies, and some armless virtuoso who performs all necessary tasks with his toes; on one lamppost hangs a manifesto announcing the appearance of Gorevaya from Berlin in the role of Mary Stuart,* a "dramatic Peter the Great"; and on another, the "divine" Antoinette Dell'era† promises the public some kind of entrechat never before seen. And right near the station hang the latest announcements: a children's show with live monkeys, races with hurdles, a new symphony, so on and so forth, too much to view, let alone to list. And so, the poor dacha husbands, compelled to amuse their wives who are bored always and everywhere, wearing their eyes out reading all these perfidious advertisements, spend their last penny and are thoroughly entangled by the extensive spider web.

My wife, thank God, is less bored than others, as a result of the exceptionally obliging nature of her cousin Bolonkin, who, in my absence, has explored the history of French naturalism with her—which, however, doesn't rescue me from fulfilling certain dacha duties. As a Pavlovsk dacha husband, I bear one of the most arduous obligations in the world: musical responsibility; no offense intended to other husbands, but I bear it serenely and without complaint. Making the usual "round-the-world cruise" past all the benches with my better

*Maria Stuarda (1835), a tragic opera in two acts by Gaetano Donizetti based on a play by Friedrich Schiller, Maria Stuart (1800).
†A well-known Italian ballerina who was the first to dance the role of the Sugar Plum Fairy.

half, and contemplating the excited and variegated sea of hats all around, I merely sigh on occasion and think to myself: "Great God above, how they *do* dress! Why on earth are they so dolled up?"

Really, what is it for? If it's to entice us men, then it's in vain: one need only listen to the first unrestricted conversation among bachelors in order to be convinced how mercilessly all these Adams make fun of the dress of these contemporary Eves. . . . If it's to entice and then to wed, it's even more useless, since one look at their extravagance quickly demolishes any erotic motivation. "No, my dear, it's too expensive—I can't afford it!" thinks the contemporary suitor, and the discouraged young lady frequently loses both all hope and her bustle at the same time. . . . Just glance at this elegant young man who's bowing and scraping with such excruciating politeness to a young woman of his acquaintance and to her mother. It seems that in another moment or two he'll offer her a formal proposal. . . . Dear mothers, don't trust this politeness; he's probably thinking to himself just what Gogol's Major Kovalyov would think upon meeting the wife of Staff-Officer Podtochkin and her daughter: "My respects, Madame! But all the same I won't marry your daughter. Thus, simply, *par amour**—if you wish!"

Alas, today every young man is without fail something like this Major Kovalyov and whether for good or ill, you can't do anything about the course of history.

And, Mesdames, you have only yourselves to blame! Why, for instance, your hats these days . . . is it really possible to wear such nonsense on your heads? A respectable young man might look at a young woman with entirely good intentions. *Not bad,* he thinks, *she'll do!* But when he glances at her hat—he throws up his hands in despair and immediately heads for the bar with

*For love (Fr.). A reference to Gogol's short story "The Nose" (1836).

a friend. So forget the young man—I'm an experienced dacha husband, and even I'm completely dumbfounded at the sight of such a fashionable enigma. One doesn't have to go far for an example—take a look at this snub-nosed blonde in the little black velvet hat with the glass beads. . . . That's no hat—heaven knows what it is! From a distance it looks just like a black cockroach that's crawled up her back and settled serenely on her upswept hairdo! And that sparkling greenish-golden hat on her companion, the savory brunette: a grasshopper, a splendid grasshopper that's accidentally jumped up on her head; and it's stuck out its little whiskers just like a grasshopper, while little sequins tremble on those whiskers just like tears—they must be her husband's tears, since he had to foot the bill for that fashion. . . . Or this faded virgin, with her sad pretension to appeal to everyone. . . . It's even difficult to say what she has on her head: it seems that some dill was sprinkled on it, and then something like peas were put on top of the dill, and on top of that grow some berries, and some little bows are sewn on next to the berries, and there's something on the bows, and the devil knows what's on this "something": it's either a red bird or something entirely indecent. Say what you will, the behavior of our ladies today is simply atrocious!

And after all this, one's surprised that the behavior of dacha children is inappropriate for their age. . . . For heaven's sake, where would they learn what's appropriate when life surrounding them is so completely inappropriate—some sort of ridiculous, extensive carnival, uninterrupted even for a minute until the first day of September,* which reminds the revelers of the approaching lean days of false learning. It's only natural that children would imitate their dear parents in all regards. One mother, for example, is in love with the first violin and seats herself, of course, on the bench just opposite him, setting her

---

*The traditional beginning of the school year.

Petya free to roam about wherever he wants. Another mother, on the contrary, is attracted by the double bassist and, fixing her lorgnette on her idol, allows her Sonya to wander around the garden until the end of the concert. Petya and Sonya, of course, don't miss out on this golden opportunity and, with all the other Petyas and Sonyas, initiate little dacha romances. Their romances are exact copies of those of their "elders," with the same casual beginnings, with the usual scenes of jealousy and cruel flirtation, and, on occasion, with the same denouements that are not quite foreseen by the school board.

A little Babylon—pure and simple!

For heaven's sake, just look around at about 11:00 P.M. on any holiday at the station platform, when the pavilions and galleries are all gaily illuminated, when the electric lamps shower blue streams of light on the enormous, motley-haired crowd, the dusty greenery, the faces, columns, flowers and hats, and in all this confusion, the gracefully resounding orchestra is being drowned out by the discordant chatter of the drearily restless dacha folks, the shrill bells of the departing train, the harsh shouts of the coachmen wandering about the station, and the hoarse cries of delight from the arriving *raznochintsy*. . . .* Babylon, if ever indeed there was one!

Around twelve midnight or later, depending on how this display of vanity concludes—a scandal, fireworks, or Gypsies, the Babylonians disperse, at long last, to their houses so that the next day they can confirm word for word everything that's written here. . . .

Where are we heading, ladies and gentlemen? Where *are* we heading?

*People of miscellaneous ranks (Rus.). In the nineteenth century the term came to be used to describe intellectuals who were not descended from aristocrats.

3

Journey to the Moon

I SHOULD TELL YOU, LADIES AND GENTLEMEN . . . I'm really embarrassed to admit it . . . but I'd never been to Arkadia before—or was it Livadia (somehow or other, impressions from both these places merge into one). In a word, I don't know how many years I've been living in Petersburg, and only yesterday did I have the honor of setting foot in one of these two sanctuaries; naturally, it was at the insistence of my wife, who explained that they were "perfectly decent places where the most diverse crowd gathers, and one would positively die of shame if any of our acquaintances found out that we hadn't been there." Let others suffer the disgrace—so, in spite of the uncertain weather, we set off.

The first impression upon our arrival in the promised land was undoubtedly striking: an imposing doorman at the entrance, elegant gentlemen dashing up from all sides on trotters, well-dressed ladies crowding near the cashier—everything indicating that you've happened onto one of those privileged locations where membership itself conveys the right to be considered an educated person. Your spirit is flattered and your gaze is won over beforehand by the brilliance and diversity that distinguish the decoration of the garden. . . . But that's only the first impression; it quickly fades, giving way to a feeling of incomprehension. . . . My wife and I managed to arrive just in time for the beginning of the performance, and following the general movement of the crowd, we wound up in front of a small, open stage on which two made-up clowns were performing a polka by whistling on ordinary combs. The select public guffawed and when the concert ended, rewarded the soloists with unanimous applause. The musicians returned from the wings with beer bottles and repeated the same polka by drumming on their bottles. A new round of applause. At the next curtain call, kitchen saucepans appeared, on which a march from *Faust* was played. All of this struck me as so incredibly stupid that I expressed to my wife my most sincere desire to return home as soon as possible. My wife looked at me as if I'd lost my mind, and silently handed me a program. I took it, glanced at the obedient faces of other husbands nearby, and submitted to my obligations.

After the soloists left the stage with their saucepans, there emerged from the wings a clumsy décolleté German woman with an elongated neck and crossed eyes; she began to produce some hoarse roulades described in the program as "A Lesson for Coquettes." The theme of these instructive couplets revolved around the tale of how one young lady, making her way from Revel* to Petersburg, lost her travel handbag in a train car and lost something else as well, even more valuable for a young lady. As repulsive as this was, it was still bearable compared to the French singer who trooped out after the traveler from Revel. She was simply infuriating. A scrawny, heavily made-up adolescent girl came rushing onto the stage wearing such a short skirt that it demolished all prejudices; in a childish voice she began to squeal some silly little song, conveying the gist for those who couldn't understand the language with her explicit gestures. . . . The foul-mouthed girl's voice could scarcely be heard over the orchestra's accompaniment, and you could merely see her winking to the disguised male stu-

*Revel is the old name in Russian for the city of Tallinn, capital of Estonia.

dents,* wiggling her bustle, and raising her legs higher than allowed by the police. Note that all this took place almost in daylight and not in some house of ill repute, but before the eyes of a so-called cultured and completely sober audience.

"Ugh, how disgusting!" I uttered almost aloud. My wife cast a perplexed glance at me and whispered in reproach: "Oh, Jean, you're so out of touch! One has to blush for you at every step."

"Excuse me, my dear, how am I so out of touch? Out of touch with what?"

"Well, with life . . . with the age . . . with what everyone is striving toward. I can't explain all this to you here in public!" she added in annoyance, and fixed her lorgnette on the repulsive French girl, who was sending a final kiss to her possessed public. . . . After such words the only thing left for me to do was to drop my eyes chastely to the program in the hope of finding there some consolation for my offended aesthetic sense. Consolation was close at hand, since the program indicated that next up was an operetta in two acts, "Revue of Gypsy Songs."

"What sort of songs are these?" I inquired of my wife, knowing that she followed the latest literature closely with the assistance of her cousin Bolonkin.

"Have you really forgotten? The same sort as we heard last year in Pavlovsk sung by Zorina. . . ."

That reminder was totally sufficient to sour me. I had never seen or heard any more vulgar and frenzied assortment in my entire life, and to hear it a second time would be a real feat. My cup of forbearance was overflowing. . . . To sit in a rustic theater for half an hour in the draft, enjoying the sight of drunken merchants who were in love with these untalented musicians was torture too excruciating for a family man, and

*Schoolboys who were required to wear their uniforms at all times and were prohibited from attending such "lewd" performances often turned up in disguise.

by the end of the first act of this idiocy, I flatly declared to my wife that I had grown too stupid during the last half hour to risk hearing the second act.

My wife, obviously satiated back in Pavlovsk by Zorina's version of a "little devil," yielded this time and hastily led me out into the fresh air to the large illuminated stage, where—in spite of the increasing dampness due to the encroaching darkness and the drizzle that had begun falling—a dazzling performance was under way. The effect on one's consciousness was truly astounding; from Sokolniki ("Gypsy Songs") you found yourself in ancient Athens, at the home of the wise Socrates and his wicked wife, Xanthippe. Before your very eyes there took place part melodrama, part panoramic ballet bearing the audacious title of "Xanthippe: Philosopher's Wife," with a mythological procession, fireworks, and Greek costumes "designed by Mlle Emilie." The spectacle, in any case, was instructive, in spite of the fact that, dripping with moisture and turning blue from the cold, these Greek men and women were shattering the illusion, reminding you of the marshy ground of Petersburg and its chronic rheumatism. In particular, the occasion when Xanthippe, irritated by the philosophical serenity of her spouse, dumped a bucket of dirty water on his bald head, made a strong impression on me. At that historical moment I unintentionally glanced at my own body, huddling from the dampness, and the excited face of my wife greedily devouring the scene with her eyes—and I arrived at an unexpected and bitter discovery—alas, the state of "warring sides" hadn't changed one bit over the last two thousand years. There was one difference: at least the Xanthippes of antiquity possessed beauty of form, while modern ones had nothing besides their perfidious bustles, under which they concealed their respect for their husbands, their conscience, and their lovers' letters. This discovery was too dispiriting not to overcome it with a strong shot of vodka; taking advantage of the goddess

Athena's imminent holiday after the ill treatment of this celebrated ancestor of dacha husbands—a holiday that absorbed all the general attention—I managed to slip out unnoticed to the buffet with the secret hope that I would manage to raise my fallen spirits as best I could before the end of the play. But my enjoyment did not last long: I'd barely managed to down a third shot when I noticed striding down the lane under an umbrella, heading right for the buffet, my implacable Marya Dmitrievna. My retreat was cut short and I candidly confessed my desertion.

"The point isn't that you'll drink any rubbish whatever," she hissed, "but that as a result of your empty-headedness, I might miss out on the mermaid!"

After those three overpowering shots and everything else I'd seen, I didn't really understand what the point was; only as a consequence of my wife's explanation that after "Xanthippe" would follow "The Mermaid," could I explain to myself the significance of the event. . . . The word *fish* suddenly reminded me: a warm dining room, a dressing gown, and an early supper in the family circle. But I managed to drive all these old-world pursuits out of my head and, opening my umbrella, hastened after my bustle-wearing lawgiver back to where I belonged.

On the rise in front of the fair booth where the underage performer had been spouting obscenities, there stood a voluminous glass box filled with hot water and illuminated from inside by an electric light. A minute later a fat lady appeared on stage, dressed all in sparkling fish scales instead of clothes, and, after greeting the audience, she crawled into this container of hot soup. What she did there, I won't say out of a feeling of squeamishness—but all the while she splashed about, the audience stared stupidly and silently, and when the lady, well stewed, climbed out of the soup onto dry land and smiled painfully in a gesture of farewell, the dissatisfied audience began to disperse. The majority, apparently, expected to witness how this venerable lady was going to be cooked right before their very own eyes. Nice mores—no doubt about it!

However, all's well when it ends, and I glanced at my watch with a much-relieved heart.

"Oho—it's twelve o'clock. Time to go home! So, my dear, do you think it's better to take a horse-drawn tram or a cab?" I said, turning to my wife. To my surprise, I noticed that she was turning green with indignation.

"Ivan Grigorevich, do you even know what you're saying? Why now it's time for *Brahma*,* do you understand, *Brrrahma*! The Italian prima ballerina about whom even Bolonkin is ecstatic, and the Nenyukovs, too, and all of our acquaintances. And suddenly you say, 'Time to leave.' No, the dampness today has left you soft in the head."

"Have mercy, my dear, why, it's already so . . ."

But my wife didn't give me a chance to finish my sentence and despotically shoved the program in my face. With the help of the electric light and assiduously protecting myself from the encroaching dampness with my umbrella, my eyes made out the following joyful news: "By public demand: The Third Scene from the Ballet *Brahma* with its brilliant décor and with the participation of the famous European ballerina Brrr . . ." I couldn't make out any more because the program was soaking wet.

"We'll seeee, we'll seeee!" I said, gritting my teeth and smiling unnaturally, and I felt that I was starting to lose my mind. . . . But at that moment a deafening bell announced to the crowd languishing near the closed theater that the mysterious *Brahma* was about to begin, and I blindly followed my waterproof other half into the free-for-all.

Although I'm by no means a graduate of the barelegged faculty, nevertheless I'll attempt to convey the details of that

*A popular ballet about the chief Hindu deity by the composer Costantino Dall'Argine (1842–77), choreographed by Hippolyte Monplaisir, and first performed at La Scala in 1868.

remarkable event. I must warn you that the theater was full to overflowing, and the audience filling it was the most exclusive ever, and its impatience to see the prima ballerina equaled the impatience of a hungry crowd in a cheap cafeteria awaiting the distribution of food.

At last the curtain went up.

The scene represented a square in front of a restaurant in the countryside. Birch trees were depicted on the rear curtain; on the proscenium, near the entrance to the restaurant, stood a table; on it, a bottle of vodka and three small glasses. The innkeeper and his wife enter and both begin to wave their arms sadly, nodding their heads to the audience, indicating that their buffet had not been doing very much business that season. But less than a minute passes when from the wings emerges a dark, elderly man wearing the clothes of an Indian prince (we guessed that this was Brahma himself), who with his gestures indicates that he is tired from his travels and wouldn't be against having a bite of supper. But the innkeeper, who's probably worked in Livadia or Arkadia before, asks such accursedly exorbitant prices that the Indian prince hesitates in indecision. At this critical moment, from the depths of the stage, an attractive, not too tall brunette appears, dressed no less scantily than the mermaid, located, apparently, at this restaurant to entice visitors, and she gestures to the innkeeper. . . . (She must be the ballerina, because at her appearance the audience shuddered and stirred.) Upon seeing the ballerina, the Indian prince forgets all economic considerations and gallantly offers her something to eat. The prima ballerina smiles approvingly and performs a graceful entrechat; rising *en pointe* and twitching her whole body, she approaches the snack on her toes. At the very same moment as she rises *en pointe,* an elderly man sitting next to me—who, up to this time had seemed to be a decent, fine-looking, and imposing fellow—suddenly seized his binoculars convulsively, and, shaking like a leaf, devoured the evildoer with his eyes, muttering in a voice choked with emotion: "Bravo, bravo, bravo!"

"Good Lord, what's the matter with him?" I inquired with genuine anxiety. "Is he in need of medical assistance?"

"Shhh," my wife replied, pulling at my sleeve with annoyance. "Don't you see that he's a balletomane? Oh, Jean, you've become so unforgivably out of touch. . . . It's simply embarrassing to be with you!"

My temporary insanity intensified, and from that point on my impressions acquired the shadow of complete confusion.

Meanwhile Madame Brahma is having a little something to eat and clinking glasses with Mr. Brahma; then, all of a sudden, right after her snack, she begins to twirl very, very quickly across the stage—I can't say definitively whether it was as a result of sudden love or the cheap vodka because I didn't have a libretto in hand. After twirling to her heart's content, unexpectedly for everyone present, she halts *en pointe* next to the prompter's box and kicks her left leg so high . . . much higher than the French adolescent . . . well, in a word, to the point where the face of the policeman in the first row twitched convulsively, as though in pain. I really can't describe what happened next in the theater. It was a genuine tempest of ecstasy, capable of darkening the strongest minds. . . . Small bouquets of flowers landed on the stage, as did a laurel wreath and something wrapped in paper. . . . My neighbor, the elderly man, suffering, according to my wife, from "balletomania," simply lost his mind: he dropped his binoculars, stamped his feet, thumped his umbrella, and, tearful with tender emotion, muttered, "Good gracious, why, it's the latest thing in science!"

When the curtain came down and the audience began to pour out of the exit, once again I heard that very same opinion from the crowd: "Today she demonstrated the *newest thing*. . . ." As a matter of fact, there was nowhere else to go!

Recovering somewhat in the fresh air and coming to myself after the extraordinary spectacle, I took advantage of the moment of illumination to ask my wife once more how she wished to return home—on a horse-drawn tram or in a cab?

"Of course, the tram," she said, sounding perplexed, "but only after we see the *trained elephant.* . . . You may do as you wish, my dear, but I definitely want to see it, or else I won't leave here. . . . The Nenyukovs praised it highly!"

I stared straight at my wife and thought one of two things: either she'd lost her mind or she was playing a joke on me. Nothing of the sort: she opened her umbrella energetically, grabbed me by the arm, and dragged me off in a direction away from the exit.

By now I had grown so numb that I really didn't care what we saw. . . . It seemed that if my wife had said to me, "My dear, I won't leave until I get to see how they decapitate a live person!" I'd have replied obediently, "Fine, my dear, let's go see how they decapitate a live person!" An elephant, a crocodile, or a person without a head—from then on it was all the same to me. . . . And so, once again we were standing in front of an open stage and among a dense forest of open umbrellas, patiently awaiting the arrival of this eighth wonder of the world. A table on the proscenium, tantalizingly set for supper, aroused the general envy of the spectators. . . . Soon from the wings a tall German appeared wearing a frock coat and a white tie, and with him followed a small, clumsy, but extremely intelligent-looking elephant that, together with the German, exchanged bows with the audience. The dignified public yawned sleepily and waited for what came next. The German draped the elephant with a dinner napkin and sat him down at the table. The elephant had a bite to eat, downed a mug of beer and, regarding the water-soaked audience before its eyes, apparently felt very satisfied with its privileged position.

"Ah, why am I not an elephant?" most likely occurred to more than one drenched husband at this moment. But nothing in life is given away for free, and when the elephant stood up from the table, the cunning German placed a stylish bicycle at its disposal, placed a jockey cap on its head, and sat its cumbersome bulk down on the small seat. The elephant frowned and drew in a deep breath. However, noting the impatience of the educated crowd, it unwillingly performed several turns around the stage on the bicycle. Approving applause could be heard from the public.

And all this past one o'clock in the morning, under pouring rain in a damp garden! Lord, how did I wind up here? Where am I? Am I on earth or on the moon? A minute later the lowered curtain started to rise again and I saw before me ice-covered mountains where some scrawny Hungarians were ice-skating. . . . There's no doubt about it—I'm on the moon.

"Is this all?" I asked my spouse feebly.

"It *seems* to be!" my spouse reassured me, glancing around not without regret at the dispersing spectators. "Thank heaven," I thought, "at last we can head for the exit."

"Well, Jean, how did you like it here?" my wife looked up at me and asked innocently.

"How did I like it?" I fastened my wandering gaze on her, and my mouth curled into a sarcastic grin. At that moment I must have looked very horrifying, because a Tartar footman standing near the exit backed away nervously at my approach. As a matter of fact I was feeling so ravenous and furious that if he'd come toward me to offer his services, I'd have torn him to pieces on the spot.

Trudging through the puddles and getting lost in the darkness among the departing carriages, we finally reached the tram and with considerable effort squeezed into its tightly packed interior. A majority of the passengers had a sleepy, exhausted look; once the tram started to move, they dozed off casually in various ambiguous poses. I was also starting to nod off but resisted energetically, shamed by the example of Marya Dmitrievna, whose face was shining with the self-satisfaction of a woman who had seen the "ultimate assertion of civilization."

"Well, how did you like it on the *moon?*" someone's voice nearby called to me.

"How can I put it . . . you'll agree that it was all somewhat strange . . . not to mention the mortifying damp. . . ."

"It's no wonder you were cold," my neighbor replied ironically. "The end of the world is approaching and the earth is naturally beginning to cool!" I *wanted* to make some objection to this odd neighbor when I suddenly felt that my limbs were growing colder, my brain was vanishing into thin air, and that I was about to plummet into an immense void with a loud noise. . . .

. . . I felt a vigorous jolt—and woke up on Mikhailovsky Square.

It was already quite light, the tram was empty, and some heavily made-up apparition with blue feathers on its head was pulling me by the collar. . . .

"Ivan Grigorevich," the apparition howled, "your behavior's simply disgraceful! When decent people are awake—you're asleep; when everyone's in raptures—you're disgusted, when . . . Well, in a word, from now on I won't set foot *with you* either in Arkadia or in Livadia . . . nowhere at all! Do you hear? Now, go find us a cab to Povarsky Lane."

The mention of Povarsky Lane immediately returns me to reality and makes it clear that before me stands my own wife and that my journey to the moon has fortunately ended.

. . . Good morning to all you dacha husbands!

4

The Dacha Husband Takes the Waters: His Diary

Caucasian Mineral Waters
Zheleznovodsk, June 23*

YESTERDAY MY WIFE AND I arrived in Zheleznovodsk and rented an apartment near the sanatorium, not far from the state hotel. But first I must tell you how I suddenly wound up taking the waters in the Caucasus instead of being in indubitable Pavlovsk. The indirect cause of my journey proved to be none other than Glavach—no matter how strange that may seem to admit—the very same good-looking Glavach who wrote nine mazurkas and who produced ninety-nine psychopathic disturbances among the circle of his symphonic lady admirers. When my wife found out definitively and reliably that Glavach wouldn't be in Pavlovsk, she suffered something like a convulsion. Coinciding with this distressing news came word of the unexpected departure abroad of our domestic friend, cousin Bolonkin; this proved to be the final blow to her fragile nerves, and my poor Marya Dmitrievna took to her bed. I summoned a specialist in women's ailments and outlined my difficult position to him frankly. The specialist examined the patient carefully and prescribed an immediate trip to take the

*A town and spa resort in the Caucasus known for its iron-rich mineral water.

waters in the Caucasus. Naturally, there was nothing to do but to request a month's vacation, to cash in a pile of five-percent banknotes in Yunker's office (my entire small savings set aside for the children), and to accompany my wife to the Caucasus.

I won't say that I was dissatisfied by such a turn of events: Petersburg with its offices and "*jours fixes,*"* its "Arkadias" and "Livadias," and Pavlovsk with its shameless bustles, pernicious cousins, and various "ninth" symphonies—all this had lately become sufficiently loathsome to me that the possibility of vacationing for a whole month in the bosom of nature filled me to the brim with hope and joy. As a matter of fact, how could this not be bliss—at long last to cast away one's rigid bureaucratic nature, to shake off for a time all the tawdry cultural rubbish that befouls our distorted lives, and to draw into oneself a deep breath of the miraculous and therapeutic mountain air! And nature, the views. . . . My God, what views! My wife and I live on the second floor and from our balcony a spectacular panorama opens up on Beshtau,† the mountains nearby, and the emerald green expanse of a thick forest grove at its foot. . . .

The one thing that spoils to some extent the poetry of the impression is the accursed prices that prevail here and the astonishing slovenliness of the apartment furnishings. At the dacha where we live, for example, there are twenty rooms in all, and from time immemorial the walls and curtains in all of them have been decorated by Caucasian flies; each resident is provided with a samovar; for domestic servants there is a drunken doorman and his pregnant wife, who addresses me as "Mr. In-patient." You can just imagine what sort of in-patient tragedies arise from all this. The other thing I don't like here is the evening gatherings on the square in front of the music pavilion. It's almost like Pavlovsk in miniature; true, there's

*Fixed days (Fr.); i.e., for receiving guests at home.
†An isolated five-domed igneous mountain near Pyatigorsk in the Northern Caucasus.

more freedom in one's haberdashery, but it's the same boring, yawn-inducing audience, the same stupidly dandyish cavaliers who exist by virtue of women's infidelity; the same marriage-destroying bustles that poison the same curative springs. . . . Oh, those bustles, those bustles! If only lightning would strike one of them sometime, thus plainly revealing a heavenly punishment for such deviation from the laws of nature!

And then there's the nasty manner in which the Caucasian residents examine women—as if they longed to undress them in their imagination. . . . Even my wife was embarrassed when some long-legged fop with a pince-nez wearing a checked suit inspected her like that. "Comme on regarde ici les femmes!"* she said to me in agitation. But I reassured her that this was undoubtedly a local custom, and that it would be risky to draw any conclusions about the waters from her first impression.

Tomorrow we'll go to see the doctor.

June 25–30

It's already been a week since my wife and I have been taking the cure according to all the rules of spa science, following the directions of Dr. Farmazonov,† recommended to my wife back in Petersburg as the specialist to consult.

Farmazonov is a local celebrity. He's no longer young and certainly not handsome, but extremely genial in his way of dealing with his patients, primarily women—a fortunate attribute, thanks to which in a short time he's made both a name and a fortune for himself. Ladies who are taking the cure simply idolize him, and if you look into his parlor during office hours, chock-full of coquettishly dressed ladies reverently whispering in anticipation of their turn, there's no way you'd ever think

*How they look at women here! (Fr.).
†The doctor's "speaking name" means "one of the Freemasons."

that you're in a doctor's waiting room; rather, you'd think you're in a temple filled with highly emotional communicants.

But, as I've already said, the doctor's kindness extends exclusively to wives taking the cure. As far as spa husbands are concerned, he shows them no indulgence whatsoever; his strict regimen ensnaring the latter is so onerous that it even produces a particular kind of illness that I've allowed myself to call "Spa-schmerz"*—something midway between "longing for the ideal" and "agony for the pocketbook." As far as I'm concerned, I began to behave like an imbecile during this period, galloping around all day like a lunging horse—from spring to spring, from the baths to the koumiss† pavilion, from the pavilion to the masseuse, and so on. I see my wife only twice a day: for dinner at noon, when she's eating and therefore hardly speaking to me; and at night, when she's sleeping. But, strongly believing in the famous miracle-working power of Caucasian waters, I bear my spa-cross with the selflessness of a genuine Christian martyr and continue to gallop around without complaint and without rest. . . . The heat is so intolerable that I feel too lazy to write any more in my diary.

July 1

The waters have already begun to do their work and have affected my wife's brain first of all. From time to time she's begun to spout nonsense about some Circassians,‡ she tosses about at night and just today suddenly declared that she wants to go horseback riding in the mountains.

*This is a play on the word *Weltschmerz* (world-pain or world-weariness), coined by the German romantic author Jean Paul (1763–1825).
†Fermented mare's milk.
‡*Circassians* is a term applied indiscriminately to all the peoples of the Northern Caucasus.

"Well, my dear, have you lost your mind completely?" I asked her. "You were always afraid to go anywhere near a horse; when we return from the theater with a cabby's old nag, you shriek at the least jolt, and now all of a sudden—you want to go riding on an Asian racer, into the mountains at that. . . . No, whatever you say, you've simply imbibed too much mineral water!"

"I haven't imbibed too much of anything, I just want to go— that's all there is to it. . . . All the ladies here go riding in the mountains—am I any worse than they are? It's all because you don't know how to ride; but that's not a good enough reason for me to have to mope about with you. . . . I want to live! Do you hear, to live, not to vegetate!" She yelled, stamped her feet, sobbed hysterically; well, it was just the same when we found out about Glavach's retirement. There was nothing to be done—we set off for the doctor. So this is how it is, I told him; what do you advise? He smiled. "Excuse me," he said, "but there's nothing dangerous about it. Let her go riding. For your serenity I can even recommend a reliable guide, one of my own acquaintances. He's accompanied more than one of my patients and the journey has always produced extremely beneficial effects." I returned home completely reassured and communicated the result of the consultation to my other half. She called me a "sweetheart," and we gladly made up. In the evening Marie and I had a merry and decorous stroll together, altogether conjugal, listening to music and laughing a great deal, while observing the local society at the spa. . . . There are so many young ladies here who look like dried-up fuchsia, even though they think they resemble Princess Mary!* How many old maids dream about the fate of Lermontov's Tamara,† how many scrofulous

*The attractive heroine in the longest section of Mikhail Lermontov's novel *The Hero of Our Time* (1840), an account of the adventures of a "superfluous man."
†The heroine of Lermontov's narrative poem *Demon* (1829–39), about the love of a fallen angel for a mortal.

gymnasium students dress up as Circassians laying claim to the role of the Demon! There are so many Yids and Yiddesses,* masseurs and cardsharps, medical doctors and people in the best of health! There are so many characters that are sick, sympathizers, sentimental and hemorrhoidal, rheumatic and pessimistic! Keep away, far away from all these types, you dacha husbands, if you don't want the curative water coursing through your veins to be instantly poisoned by the worst venom that ever existed in the whole wide world—mineral water gossip.

That's why I refrain from all spa acquaintanceships and was extremely dissatisfied when two gaunt young men with monocles—wearing blue jackets and yellow clodhoppers, of the pernicious breed called "dacha gophers"—exchanged greetings with my wife; what's more, I clearly heard one of them whisper into the other's ear, "Look over there: it's a dacha husband!" I almost made a rude gesture, but my wife informed me that they were perfectly decent young men; besides, one of them was an excellent poet, the other a brilliant artist. I kept my silence that time, although, to confess, I didn't notice any signs of genius in their good-for-nothing faces.

We returned from the concert earlier than usual, since tomorrow I must catch the first stagecoach to Pyatigorsk and spend the whole day carrying out various errands for my wife.

July 3

Yesterday it was already late in the evening when I returned from my trip. . . . Loaded down with the boxes and packages that always figure in contemporary spousal relations, exhausted, dusty, and half-crazy from the intense heat in Pyatigorsk that almost overcame me, I ran upstairs to my room and tried to get in . . . it was locked. I asked the doorman where my wife

*Derogatory terms for Jews are unfortunately quite common in Russian literature.

was. The half-drunk doorman smiled foolishly and replied in a completely barbaric dialect something of this sort: "She went off to climb Beshtau and still hasn't made it back." A terrible premonition invaded my heart: the unbalanced woman insisted on getting her own way and had gone riding in the mountains, had fallen off her horse and broken her leg, if she hadn't fractured even more, and was most likely now lying somewhere in a prolonged faint. . . . I hurriedly deposited my purchases in the doorman's arms and headed for the park in an attempt to learn something about my headstrong other half. . . . The music had ended some time before, and there were very few people left in the square. . . . I turned onto the main avenue and bumped right into the brilliant good-for-nothing fellows in their yellow clodhoppers.

"You're probably looking for your wife?" they asked, noticing my agitated face.

"Mmm . . . yes . . . more or less!" I muttered, extremely irritated.

"She's over there at the spa . . . with Mikhail!" the younger loafer reported with a sly smile.

"At the spa . . . with Mikhail?" I cried joyfully. The monocles exchanged ambiguous glances and snickered right in my face. But, heartened by the comforting news, I let the inappropriate mockery fly past and rushed over to "Mikhail's spring" at full speed. I reached the spring, went through the arch—there was nobody there! It suddenly occurred to me that my wife had already consumed her water and was now strolling in the Mikhailovsky gallery. . . . I rushed over there and, after racing up the stairs, suddenly turned into a pillar of salt: on a bench, in the depths of the gallery, sat my very own wife, Marya Dmitrievna, in a coquettishly blue riding outfit, and next to her, in the pose of Lermontov's Demon . . . sat some dark-skinned man wearing an elegant Circassian coat, a fur hat, and a dagger in his belt. . . . I wanted to say something, but my tongue didn't obey and some sort of hoarse whistling sound emerged from my chest. . . . My wife saw me, jumped up from the bench, and extended her arms to me, as if for an embrace: "Jean . . . at last! Did you bring what I asked you to? Ah, how nice it all is!" And she clung to my shoulder. But I pushed her away coldly, and with the dignity of an offended husband, asked her first of all to explain what role in this comedy the dark stranger had played.

"This is my savior!" she cried ecstatically. "If it weren't for him, you would never have seen your little Marya alive on this earth!" And hurriedly, anxiously, amid constant hesitation and blushes, she explained to me that, as a result of the "doctor's prescription," she had been planning to go for a ride in the mountains; she had invited Mikhail Abramovich, who had been recommended to serve as her guide, and now she thanked heaven that fate had sent him to her. While descending the summit of Beshtau, her horse had stumbled and she probably would have sailed off into the gorge, had it not been for Mikhail Abramovich's chivalry. He grabbed her at the very moment things had gone dark before her eyes, and carefully brought her down to the foot of the mountain on his own mount. There she came to, and now she felt just fine. "Yes," she concluded with tears in her voice, "I owe him my life . . . do you understand, Jean, my life! Why don't you thank him?" she whispered to me in irritation, and with a glance, summoned Mikhail Abramovich from where he was standing at a distance, squinting enviously. I muttered something as a sign of gratitude and hesitantly extended my hand to the handsome mountain dweller. . . . He bared his teeth indifferently, raised his fur hat, and in a thin, guttural voice uttered: "For heaven's sake . . . anything in my power!" At this difficult moment, someone burst out laughing behind my back; turning around, I saw those familiar good-for-nothings in their blue trousers, exchanging greetings with my wife. Although all's well that ends well, in this case the scene had concluded in an unattractive manner, and I voiced my concerns to my wife upon our return. Unexpectedly my wife became completely enraged: "Not only are you a despot, you're simply a monster!" she shrieked when I expressed myself scornfully about her dubious knight. "A man risks his life to save your own wife, and still you have the nerve to mock him! What on earth could that mean? Perhaps you'd have preferred it if I'd tumbled into the gorge? Answer me directly: would you, would you, would you?"

I kept silent after her last question and, feeling infernally exhausted from the trip, begged to postpone the discussion until morning.

July 4

If it's said, "Morning light is always wiser than the night," in the present instance the morning light turned out to be so wise that I simply don't know how to relate the events.

After waking and consuming some coffee according to our Petersburg habits, we separated until dinner, each of us going about his or her own spa business. The morning was too delightful to argue, and we parted in relative peace, not suspecting what sort of surprise was in the making for our family accord. It must be said that while still strolling along the station platform listening to the morning music, several of the people taking the cure regarded me with special curiosity, but knowing that all spa guests in general look rather strange, I didn't pay the least attention to the usual mineral water gossip. The matter was clarified only before dinner, when, while looking for my wife in all the remote spa corners, I glanced in passing into the Mikhailovsky gallery. My wife wasn't there, but my attention was attracted for some reason by a large poster hanging on the wall with the figure of a devil in bold type, as it first seemed to me as a result of my nearsightedness. I went up closer to examine the announcement, most likely promising some traveling magician . . . and what did I see? Instead of the devil—my own portrait drawn in pencil with horns and amazing goggle eyes; trembling with indignation, I read the following verses printed below:

The Bewilderment of the Dacha Husband

Yesterday I unexpectedly came upon my wife
In a remote gallery with a Circassian,
Whom, it seems, a doctor had prescribed
To cheer her up at the spa.

At first, I confess, I was offended
By his impudent, bellicose mug,
But I soon discovered that he himself was the "spring . . ."
And that his name was . . . Mikhail.

Then I felt resigned and shook the hand
Of this salutary son of nature,
And I groaned with secret sadness in my soul:
"So that's why the doctor prescribed to my wife
The splendid waters of the Caucasus."

I devoured line after line as if they were quinine pills and could hardly believe the vile lampoon with my own eyes. . . . What on earth was going on? Is it possible so impudently and openly to make such fun of marriage, conjugal honor, and the highest human value—love? Where are we heading? Ladies and gentlemen, I ask you once again, where are we heading? Why, soon it will get to the point where lovers will be dispensed by doctors' prescriptions directly from the pharmacy, like some sort of infusion of valerian or licorice. . . . Oh, what mores, what mores!

Of course I immediately ripped the loathsome caricature off the wall and rushed right to the commissioner. But reconsidering along the way, I realized that such a step would lead to unnecessary publicity; I turned away from the commissioner's office and headed in the direction of our apartment. My wife was at home, changing for dinner from her bathing peignoir into some lace madness.

"Why do you have such a funny look on your face?" my buoyant other half inquired upon seeing me.

I glanced up at her with a sinister look and handed her the "spa affair."

She quickly skimmed the lampoon, nervously chewing on her lower lip—either because of anger or out of suppressed laughter, and, with a tinge of irony, she drawled: "What exactly do you intend to do?"

"And you have the nerve to ask me what do I intend to do? Naturally uncover this vile versifier and give him a good thrashing; if I don't manage to discover who it is and give him a thrashing—and I certainly have my suspicions about who initiated this whole intrigue—I will summon your spa Circassian to a duel and squash him like a cockroach."

My wife burst out laughing right in my face.

"Couldn't you think of anything more foolish?" she asked, looking me up and down with a contemptuous glance.

Overwhelmed by such bustle-indifference, I felt totally at a loss.

"And in your opinion just what should I do?" I asked in a despondent voice. "I'm too ashamed to show myself now in Zheleznovodsk. Everyone will laugh at me!"

"There's nothing to do but to get away from here without a moment's hesitation. At first, perhaps to Kislovodsk, then to Petersburg, back to your department."

"And what about you . . . will you come with me?"

"Naturally, I'll follow you . . . after I've completed my course of treatment . . . no sooner, of course. . . ."

"What do you mean, after your course of treatment?"

"Very simply, when I've completed my full course of treatment at the spa," she added with irritation. "I still have twenty glasses of Mikhail's spring water to drink and twenty more Baryatinsky baths to take. However, I have no time to philosophize with you—I want to eat. . . . Are you coming to dinner or not?"

I felt exasperated.

"Thank you kindly. Your philosophy has driven away my appetite."

"Each to his own philosophy. I don't plan to starve myself as a result of your nearsightedness. Who's to blame, when all's said and done, for this whole business, if not you yourself?"

"Me? I'm to blame?"

"Yes, you're to blame! What decent spa husband would follow a course of treatment in the same group as his wife? In addition to constraint and scandal, nothing else can come of it. You should have realized this some time ago. Good-bye!" And, rustling her freshly starched skirt in indignation, she left the room.

I gazed in silence after my depraved other half, grabbed my head in despair, and just as I was dressed, in my magnificent Panama hat and my new Petersburg suit, I threw myself face-down on the bed and lay there until evening without moving and without dinner in a dull stupor: why the devil did I get married?

July 8

Tomorrow I will emigrate to Kislovodsk. I've spent these last three days in seclusion, not venturing to take a single step outside my room, in spite of the tropical heat, and ordering dinner from the neighboring eating-house. As it turns out, the vile lampoon had already managed to circulate in copies among those taking the cure, and it earned cheap laurels for the adulterous artists. Complete strangers inquired of the servants about my health; my wife became an object of general curiosity. In a word, a full-blown scandal had erupted. Marya Dmitrievna, however, was in no way shocked by this disgraceful attention: women, as is well known, strive by both direct and indirect means to attract attention to themselves. It goes without saying that I terminated all useless altercations with her, postponing serious discussion until we got back to Petersburg. Let her complete her course of mineral water enlightenment successfully—I finished my own sooner than I had expected!

Yessentuki* Station, July 9, morning

During the course of my journey I distracted myself by reading various medical brochures about Caucasian mineral water that had been purchased by my wife for my consolation. . . . My God, how they love each other—these dear doctors! What touching agreement prevails among them on all questions regarding spa practice! Dr. Vodopyanov,† for example, writes about Dr. Perepyanov's‡ brochure in the following way: "He [Perepyanov] demonstrates that hydrogen sulfide deoxidizes phosphoric acid and alkaline salts and converts them into sulfurous compounds. We refuse even to argue with such a charlatan. . . . He belongs in a mental institution, and not in . . . ," and so on. And Dr. Perepyanov retorts to his opponent with the following contention: "The absence of proper upbringing is apparent on every page of Dr. Vodopyanov's brochure. One must possess a high degree of impudence and arrogance to write such nonsense about the absorption of minerals. . . ." I picked up a third brochure by a much less polemical nature— a well-known essay by our dearest Farmazonov, "The Magical

---

*Town in the Stavropol region located at the base of the Caucasian Mountains.
†The "speaking name" Vodopyanov means "drunk on water."
‡The "speaking name" Perepyanov means "drunk once again."

Qualities of Kislovodsk," and opened it to the chapter entitled "The Advantage of Kislovodsk Air." This advantage was depicted in the following words:

> The impact of mountain air here is striking: patients suffering from consumption who have lost huge amounts of blood, who can hardly drag their own legs and for whose recovery all hope has been lost—blossom like roses within one week, and after a month they can compete with wild goats in their agility to run through the mountains. And Narzan water?* Its stimulating effect is so powerful that even important government officials, after tasting this bubbly liquid, become relaxed and feel at ease. The most hopeless hypochondriac, after bathing in Narzan water, turns into a wit and a Don Juan. I'm not even talking about ladies: restrained in Pyatigorsk, condescending in Zheleznovodsk, they are transformed into genuine Messalinas†—playful sparks appear in their eyes and their pale cheeks are enflamed by a bright, lustful blush.

It didn't get any easier with every passing hour. Well, if the doctors in their own scientific brochures attest to such influence, what's left for us husbands to do but shrug our shoulders?

Kislovodsk, July 10, morning

Upon arrival in Kislovodsk, I checked into the family suite (!) at the "Spa Guests' Leisure Hotel," unpacked my things, found my diary, and ordered some supper. The servant who delivered my lamb cutlets seemed like a sensible lad and I took advantage

---

*Narzan mineral water has been associated with Kislovodsk in the Northern Caucasus for more than a century.

†Messalina (ca. 22–ca. 48), the third wife of the Emperor Claudius, is often described as an insatiable nymphomaniac.

of the situation to confirm the accuracy of Dr. Farmazonov's panegyric to Kislovodsk.

"Well, how are things here . . . is everything *satisfactory*?" I inquired, a little embarrassed, implying, of course, the question of "spousal" satisfaction. Apparently, this cunning native of Kislovodsk didn't understand my hint or didn't want to, and silently shifted his weight from one foot to the other. Then I explained to him directly—that for several reasons I was extremely interested in *just how* ladies amuse themselves here—and handed him a ruble note. Probably the lackey took me for some spa bon vivant, because he shook his head sympathetically, squinted his eyes slyly, and at once began to chat informally.

"It's well known how," he said with a sly grin. "They be 'takin' the cure.' What else they be doin' here, but 'takin' the cure'. . . ? It gits to be a scandal, don't it, with them . . . them rascals in their fancy fur hats. . . ."

"What rascals?"

"Them's the ones that pose as Circassians; but in their own way, these ladies don't turn their noses up even at ord'nary soldiers, 'specially these ones from the military band, if they're wearin' even fancier fur hats. . . . I never understand, sir, what they see in 'em. Why, if we're talkin' 'bout it now, pick a Russian, any one; that fella still goes to the bathhouse, while these ones in their dumb fur hats smell like horses, given the way they lives their lives—it's jes' awful to see."

"But the ladies must like something about them!" I ventured, forcing a smile.

"They're very rough in their love-makin', sir, that's what I think it is. Ya don't have to go far—why, right here, jes' year before last, the wife of a rich merchant from Moscow was stayin' in room number ten, and she had a very nasty affair. . . ."

"Oh . . . what happened?" I asked absentmindedly, already sufficiently disturbed by the previous information.

"She goes and falls for a Kabardian,* fella from the musicians' cooperative, a real dark-haired one, a sly fox, he was; well, everything be a-goin' fine and dandy, she be 'takin' the cure' well enough. But thing is, she's got a weak char'cter and soon took a likin' to another fella . . . a fair-haired one. And the first one catches her with his mate at Krestovaya Mountain and gives her such a whippin' for her betrayal that she can't even crawl out of her room for four days and four nights. And what do ya know, sir," he concluded, spreading his hands in perplexity, "she likes it. . . . She follows that fella to his mountain village. Needless to say, he robs her blind and sends her packin' at the New Year's. Then he buys hisself a herd o' horses with her money and now he's a-livin' high off the hog, jes' like a Crimean khan."

"Why, the devil knows what's going on if only you're not lying, you scoundrel!" I protested, glancing suspiciously into the eyes of this talkative raconteur.

"If ya please, sir, why should I lie? Ya think I'm some sort of joker in a dumb fur hat? Stay here with us a little while and ya'll see for yourself. Just look over there," he winked at me mysteriously, leading me over to the window and opening it cautiously. "Jes' below us, room number one, where the lieutenant's wife be stayin', right after the concert, the flute player comes in to visit her. Well then, sir, I be tellin' ya the truth, or what?"

As a matter of fact, a minute later a stately figure in a tall fur hat appeared in the lane and, after an agreed-upon signal, casually climbed in through a window that opened with a squeak. I now regarded my informant with some trepidation, like the latest Columbus who had discovered an America unknown to me.

"And, along this here corridor, jes' two rooms over, the wife of a landowner from Tambov also be 'takin' the cure.' A horse

*The Kabardians are a tribe of Northern Caucasians.

lover from Kislovodsk comes in to drink tea with her every evenin' after the public's gone and left the hotel. One can say they'll part very soon. Why, there they are, speak of the devil, over there, more to the left. . . ." I glanced to the left, in the direction of the second floor, and saw in the deep twilight a tall fur hat descending the stairs from the balcony. . . .

This was beyond all my expectations, and I hastily handed my Columbus a three-ruble note—hoping that he'd take himself off to the devil. Completely mortified, I collapsed onto the sofa in front of my cold lamb cutlets. "My God, what will happen, what on earth will happen?" my lips mumbled softly. . . . I don't know what I would've done to myself in such a fit of hopeless pessimism, if a savior hadn't come to my rescue—namely, sleep, which soon overtook me on that very same sofa—though I was still hungry, tired, and half-mad from all these moral torments.

July 10–15

These last few days I've been wandering around Kislovodsk and its environs like a lost soul, almost without paying attention to the surrounding commotion at the spa and the mountain splendors displayed on all sides. My vacation ends next week, and I've been entirely engrossed by an ominous thought—would my dearest other half follow me back to Petersburg, or, distracted by the powerful Narzan tendency, would she insist on pursuing the full course of her mineral water treatment? One thing was now clear to me: I had jumped from the frying pan right into the fire. In Petersburg with its *jours fixes* and its Arkadias, and in Pavlovsk with its symphonies and cousins, in spite of all the perversions of local life, certain rules of human decorum had still not lost their force, and to a certain extent, had restrained the "bustle-demon" that held sway over today's women. Here in the Caucasus, where, following the example of Lermontov's "Demon," the Fall was enshrined in legend, the bustle-demon felt right at home. In fact, before whom can these bustle-wearing women feel ashamed? Their husbands? But they rarely accompany their wives here, and these days the wives feel least of all ashamed in front of their husbands. The conventions of society? But they don't exist here; instead, people are surrounded only by majestic, mute mountains, the same ones that were so indifferently silent when Russian men perished during wartime; and naturally, now they won't recount to anyone how our wives perish in peacetime. Oh, Caucasus, Caucasus, it was not in vain that our poets christened you "fatal!"

"Will she or won't she follow me?" I asked myself like Hamlet, wandering from one corner of the Narzan gallery to the other, inhaling its fatal, numbing atmosphere. "Well, and if she doesn't follow me, would it really make any difference? After all, it isn't she who looks after our children; the governess Angela Fyodorovna does that. . . . Why, I never get to enjoy my legal rights, while all those 'fancy fur hats' do. So, I ask myself, what am I worrying about? Why should I rack my brains so helplessly, for what reason do I torment myself, and suffer as a result of this unbalanced, disturbed, bustle-wearing, superficial creature? Could it be that in spite of all our dacha and spa misfortunes, I'm still somewhat attached to this heartless, worthless fashion plate? It's odd, damn it!"

July 17

Yesterday I received a short note from my wife informing me that she was heading for Kislovodsk on the morning stagecoach, and today I had the pleasure of beholding her in person with my own eyes—a little plumper, more invigorated, and, if I'm not mistaken (given today's improved cosmetics, mistakes are more than possible), somehow more attractive. After our initial greeting, rather more affectionate than expected, she communicated to me some rather sensational news: the two Ajaxes* (as the fellows in blue trousers and fancy fur hats were called) had quarreled and were no longer together: the younger one had stolen from the older the wife of a wealthy Moscow merchant, whom both had been courting at first, and now he was considered her official spa suitor. A Georgian schoolboy from Tbilisi, who had so amused the ladies with his diffidence, had been taken on "to be educated" by General Z.'s wife, and the Armenian Princess K. was enamored of "Don Quixote" (who would've expected it!), the same consumptive cyclist who dragged a two-wheel bicycle with him from Petersburg and who'd been cursing the Caucasus because of its uneven roads, and so on and so forth. In a word, she let loose a whole stream of news that was as interesting to me as ballet gossip would be to a monk.

"You're chattering so much, Marie, but you haven't told me the most important thing," I said, scolding her. "Did you have a good trip?"

"Oh, wonderful. . . . There was a group of people from Zheleznovodsk . . . Madame Shalashnikova, General Bestsenny's wife, a red-haired widow, and all of them, of course, with their admirers. . . . And what views, Jean, simply charming! And imagine, what a happy coincidence: in Yessentuki Mikhail Abramovich joined us as well . . . *souviens-tu* . . .† my savior from Zheleznovodsk. . . . Ah, I was so glad to have the chance to thank him once more!"

I remained silent so as not to spoil our pleasant reunion, although I could plainly see that my wife was lying about the innocence of the Yessentuki coincidence. Just you wait, Marya Dmitrievna, wait till we get to Petersburg. We'll have a real heart-to-heart!

---

*In Greek mythology Ajax, a hero of the Trojan War, was a huge man, slow of thought and speech, but very courageous.
†You remember (Fr.).

Narzan, like any water with iron, had affected her mind first of all. The idea that occurred to her today surpasses all probability. . . . Just imagine what she suddenly conceived: to go horseback riding on Bermamut* to see the sunrise! That was a trip of more than forty versts,† through treacherous ravines; besides, half the journey would have to be done at night, amidst all sorts of unforeseen dangers!

Needless to say, a stormy scene took place between us.

After hesitating a long time about whether to remind my wife about our impending departure and thus instantly sober her up from her spa intoxication, I finally plucked up my courage and explained to her—not without difficulty, mind you—that my vacation would end the day after tomorrow and that we must immediately depart without fail that very day, for which decision I presented various reasons—financial, social, and familial. Obviously, swept away by the decisiveness of my tone, she seemed so completely distraught at first that it was painful even to look at her, but this vague awareness of her duty didn't last long; she suddenly remembered something and at that moment her face turned a bright color, and she became as irritated and agitated as Narzan water.

"Leave? The day after tomorrow? You want to leave here the day after tomorrow? Ivan Grigorevich, are you in your right mind? Leave the day after tomorrow? That's a fine how-do-you-do! That's what I call genuine conjugal courtesy!" And my wife burst into hysterical laughter.

I stood my ground.

"Don't you know what the day after tomorrow is?" she wheezed, flaring her nostrils in indignation.

"Wednesday, my angel," I replied softly.

---

*A mountain located near Kislovodsk with an altitude of 8,500 feet.
†A Russian measure of length equal to 0.66 miles.

"The day after tomorrow is my name day!"* she moaned indistinctly.

I was a little embarrassed, but pointed out to her that we could share a family dinner together that day in Kislovodsk, and still depart in the evening.

I don't know what I said that was so offensive by proposing a family dinner, but my Marya Dmitrievna turned into a real shrew.

"I don't want any of your café dinners," she howled, "nor any of your old-fashioned celebrations, your sloppy sentimentality, I don't want anything. . . . If we're going to celebrate my name day in the Caucasus, then we'll do so in a fitting manner . . . somewhere on a summit . . . in the clouds . . . in the bosom of pristine nature." She screwed up her eyes, her face turned red, and she suddenly became subdued. "You know, Jean, for my name day I don't need any present, only that you allow me . . . to go riding on Bermamut—to see the sunrise. The Nenyukovs say that to be in the Caucasus and not see Mount Elborus† at sunrise—is like being in Rome and not seeing the pope. . . . Mikhail Abramovich, most likely, would agree to take me there by the shortest possible route. . . . Say you'll let me go! You will, my dear, won't you?" And her face assumed that gently imploring expression that bustle-wives use only three times a year: Good Friday, the night before Christmas, and New Year's Eve.

In spite of the regularity of excursions to Bermamut among spa guests, I was suddenly overcome by some ominous premonition and replied with composure: "If you absolutely insist . . . so be it, my friend . . . only I shall go, too . . . together with you!"

My wife's face winced nervously.

*The birthday or feast day of the saint for whom a person is named, celebrated as birthdays are in the West.
†Elborus or Elbrus (18,510 feet), located in the Northern Caucasus, is the highest peak on the European continent.

"If you absolutely insist on spoiling the poetry of my journey with your conjugal grumbling . . . then come along. . . . I didn't invite you in the interest of your own health!"

"One excursion won't result in any great injury. . . ."

"And so, you positively insist on coming with us. . . . Is that your last word?"

"That's my last word!" I uttered firmly, my insides growing cold as a result of my own bravery.

"You've remained the same kind of despot here in the Caucasus as you always were in Petersburg. The waters haven't had the least impact on you!"

"On the other hand, they've had too strong an impact on you!" I retorted.

She snorted indignantly, feverishly wrapped herself up in some foolish cloak, and disappeared from the house until evening.

Taking advantage of her absence, I procured a sheet of paper and wrote my domestic spiritual testament in case of my death during the excursion to Elborus. At the same time I swore a solemn oath to myself—from tomorrow on, never to allow my unruly wife out of my sight even for a minute, right up until our departure for Petersburg.

Moscow, July 29

I am recording these last lines in Moscow in a desolate and nasty room of a cheap hotel. I record them with an uneasy and pathetic hand, a grieving heart, and a mind that has yet to recover from the overwhelming impressions of the recent catastrophe. Yes, ladies and gentlemen, an incident occurred that is unheard of and unseen in the chronicles of spousal cohabitation, exceeding all human probability, an event that can be called "historic" to some extent. In view of the final significance of the recent disaster, I shall temporarily stash my spousal pride in my pocket and, as a lesson to my descendants, relate all the outstanding circumstances of my spa odyssey. As you already know, I had definitely decided to make the journey to Mount Elborus with my wife and her questionable knight. What my heroism cost me will be revealed below.

We left on the eve of my wife's name day, that is, on the twenty-first of July in the evening. For my part, I took precautions to protect my person from all meteorological and miscellaneous conditions that might occur during the course of our extraordinary forty-verst journey—on horseback, at night, through unpopulated locales. I wore a felt cloak and a fur hat, and took along my revolver, an umbrella, an extra pair of eyeglasses, and a pack of Swedish matches; I applied cold cream where necessary and stashed a package of quinine in the rear pocket of my jacket. My wife took nothing with her except her frivolousness, but her obliging spa prince hoisted an entire suitcase up to his saddle, not counting his two saddlebags bursting at the seams with all sorts of provisions.

In general this prince behaved in an enigmatic manner: first, he hardly said one word to me, pleading shakiness in his spoken Russian; second, he kept exchanging some mysterious signals with my wife, pointing toward the east; and finally, he led us not by the direct stagecoach road, but by some incomprehensible zigzags with various bewildering descents, along the edge of appalling precipices, as if he were intentionally testing my Petersburg nerves. My wife continually shouted to me according to the guide's instructions: "Jean, be careful, here's a sheer drop!" "Jean, drop the reins, we're about to ford a mountain stream!" And do you think that was everything? There were packs of wolfhounds that threatened us with their ferocious barking every time we rode past a Karacheevan* or Kabardian camp! There were various dark-skinned people on

---

*Another tribe of Northern Caucasians.

horseback whom we encountered from time to time and who my wife, in her innocence, assumed were Dzhigits!* And then the terrible downpour with thunder that overtook us midway and that seemed to me to constitute genuine agony in the mountains, ready to wipe our entire ridiculous party off the face of the earth! And the intolerable pain in my legs, spine, and more, as a result of my being unaccustomed to riding on horseback! I can't possibly list everything. "Oh, night of torments!" I can boldly exclaim together with Pushkin's Kochubey.† At last we arrived.

That is, strictly speaking, we suddenly wound up in some indistinguishable wilderness in an unmitigated realm of impenetrable, cold, and mysterious fog. The road to Mount Bermamut ends with an elevated ravine, blocked in front by a monstrous precipice; according to my wife, we were now located precisely on the designated raised area. We dismounted our horses, and once again my wife cordially warned me not to budge from that place because, as a result of the thick fog, it was decidedly impossible to determine on which side the precipice was located, and every step to the side could threaten one's demise. I thanked her for this pleasant news and stretched out on the ground like a sheet, scarcely breathing from my exhaustion. Meanwhile it was getting a little brighter, and although the silhouette of Mount Elborus was only indistinctly illuminated ahead behind a curtain of fog, it was sufficiently light on the raised area, so I could clearly discern traces of pink powder on my spouse's face. The prince drew from his saddlebag a bottle of cognac, some cheese, butter, and rolls, and all three of us amicably had a little something to eat. Slowly I began to feel

---

*Caucasian horsemen.

†Vasily Kochubey (ca. 1640–1708) was a Ukrainian nobleman and statesman who became a close associate of the Cossack Hetman (military commander) Ivan Mazepa. Alexander Pushkin romanticized his story in the poem *Poltava* (1828).

warmer, and my spirits were revived. But that didn't last long. A wind came up and the fog ahead once again enveloped the raised area, but now to such an extent that I completely lost sight of my wife, our guide, and our meal. . . . "Are you still here?" I called out, scared stiff, to my comrades-in-arms. . . .

"Shhh . . . look ahead . . . the sun is coming up!" said someone's distant voice. The fog was becoming thicker and thicker. I was getting ready to call out to them a second time, but suddenly I heard something between a whistle and a moan. I was just about to rush off in the direction of this strange sound, but I suddenly recalled my wife's warning, that death was lurking behind each and every unnecessary step. . . . Feeling a bit stupefied by an extra shot of cognac, the fog, and the unfamiliar impressions, I vaguely cast my gaze into space and froze in place in anticipation of the sunrise. . . . And sure enough, the sun appeared. . . .

It rose over Mount Elborus—blinding, serene, majestic, as it climbed higher and higher; stretched out beneath, surrounded by morning mist, the Bermamut valley awoke and stirred. . . . When the sun stood high in the cloudless firmament, sparkling with millions of rays over the pearly chain of mountains, the curtain of clouds, obscuring the surroundings, parted as if by magic—and the Caucasus appeared to my sight in its genuine, terrifying immensity, in all its wild and irresistible splendor. . . . It was a picture that overwhelms all description, raises the spirits, and soothes the heart, leaving somewhere down below, on the bottom of the dark precipice, various trivial human afflictions. . . .

"Marie, look, what a spectacular sight!" I exclaimed in ecstasy. "Doesn't this divine panorama elevate and cleanse the soul? Why, it's . . ." Tears dropped spontaneously from my eyes beneath my glasses and, feeling distraught, I fell to my knees. . . .

"Marie . . . just look!"

There was no reply.

I turned my head in perplexity. The fog, covering the raised area, had dispersed, but on the raised area there was no Marie, no guide, and no horses. . . .

"Wife . . . Marya Dmitrievna!" I cried in a frenzy.

Not a sound.

My heart started to pound. *The poor unfortunates have tumbled into the abyss!* was my first thought. *The moaning that I heard was, most likely, her last marital farewell. . . . But, what about our horses? And where's our food? Could it also have fallen into the abyss?* I took a few steps forward and there, not far off in the distance, I saw my trusty steed grazing peacefully on some mountain moss; next to him, lying at his feet . . . the discarded bustle of my treacherous spouse's dress. . . .

Now there was absolutely no doubt at all—*they had run away* . . . and I was left all alone, at the whim of fate, in the middle of this magnificent desolation! This unexpected discovery was so obvious and simultaneously so awful that for the first few moments I stood there rooted to the spot, staring distractedly at the majestically indifferent Elborus, and then at the perfidious bustle lying at my feet. At last I grabbed the bustle and hurled it indignantly into the precipice, to the distress of the birds of prey; besides, I wanted to say something in reproach to that old onlooker Elborus, but all my strength left me, and breaking down in tears, I threw myself down pathetically on the grass. . . .

I don't know how long I lay there in that position—but when I raised my head I saw before me a completely unexpected sympathizer—a huge, snow-white Bermamut eagle sitting on the adjacent summit. The eagle looked at me with sadness and a lack of comprehension, just as if it wanted to say: "Ah, a dacha husband—I never expected to see you! How on earth did you wind up here?" I doffed my hat and politely thanked him for his touching concern.

However, I was so distraught that I hardly knew what I was doing, and subsequent events are lost in a total obscurity. I vaguely recall that after futile searching and calling, I mounted my horse and gave him his head; I remember that my fine steed carried me to some shaggy shepherd, who in turn drove me, more dead than alive, in his creaky cart to Kislovodsk.

What else is there to tell? I waited in our room for my wife for three days and three nights; after enduring that ordeal, I returned to Petersburg. The facts were obvious: she, just like the wife of that Moscow merchant, had run off with that rogue to his village. I decided to conceal my Caucasian catastrophe from friends and relatives for a time because, you'll agree, in my position as a state counselor, it was somehow embarrassing to admit that I'd accidentally lost my own wife. . . .

One more melancholy detail:

When I boarded the train at the Mineral Waters station and it moved off, I noticed in the middle of the car some faded and pinched figure, undoubtedly male, wearing a raincoat and a hat pulled down over his eyes; as soon as the train had pulled far enough away from the station, he suddenly leaned out of the window and shook his fist indignantly at the Caucasian mountains. This gesture seemed peculiar to me, and, at the same time, I took an immediate liking to this stranger! I sat next to this mountain hater and inquired where he was going.

"Petersburg . . . to the consistory* . . . to plead for a divorce!" he muttered, glowering at me sullenly and distrustfully. A few words were entirely sufficient for us to deduce each other's identity: here was another dacha husband who'd also lost his wife . . . on the *Crimean peninsula,* somewhere near the town of Alupka, and who was returning in a roundabout way to his homeland.

We both cried out in sympathy and embraced each other with a loud, pitiful wail. A commotion erupted in the train car.

*A church tribunal or governing body empowered to grant divorces.

Passengers jumped up from their seats and rushed over to us to find out what was the matter. Everyone thought a train wreck had occurred. But we kindly explained to those who were curious that something even more alarming had occurred: *the wreck of marital happiness.* The passengers calmed down at once, exchanged uncomprehending glances with one another, and apathetically returned to their own seats.

*Finita la commedia!**

---

*The comedy is ended (It.). A reference to Lermontov's novel *A Hero of Our Time* (1837–40), in which Pechorin utters these words upon seeing the body of a man he has slain in a duel.

5

The Philosophy of the Dacha Husband

AND SO, IT CAME TO PASS . . . from being a dacha husband I found myself entirely unexpectedly in the ambiguous position of a "bustle-widower." . . . Which one of the two conditions was more offensive, I'm unable to decide calmly now, because all this time I've been suffering from an attack of deepest pessimism. As a matter of fact, why do I go on living? Why was I born? Why did I marry? Tell me, please, what this completely insane, harried maelstrom is all about, the one in which we pure intellectuals* wear ourselves out indefatigably, never having a moment's peace to catch our breath or reckon how many pounds of human dignity we've wasted on all this idiotic pandemonium. Moreover, it's reached the point where we have so many things to do that we can barely snatch time to have dinner or get a good night's sleep, where urgent, pressing business leads exclusively to achieving the most "comfy" living conditions, where in the agitated pursuit for such, life itself, real life, passes through our fingers absolutely unnoticed, just like a dream. Yes, yes, we all need ambience, ambience most of all— luxurious, dazzling, astonishing; such an ambience is inevitably necessary, because our ambience-conscious wives become more and more demanding every year, and they become more demanding because . . . but there's the hitch, a very nasty hitch, up against which husbands' strongest minds stumble and fall!

*That is, members of the Russian intelligentsia.

I shall begin my confession with the fact that I got married just like everyone else did, that is, simply because after the age of thirty, it's said that in order not to violate social convention, one must absolutely marry. But whom? Naturally, a woman of one's own social circle . . . that is to say, a woman with a bustle. I married a woman with a bustle because, of the three evils into which, in my opinion, the female realm is subdivided, the last one seemed to me to be the most tempting. These three misfortunes are as follows: (1) women of letters, (2) women of the stove, and (3) women of the bustle. In the first category I include . . . women—oh, it's even too awful to say—women students and other supposedly independent creatures; I always smile pessimistically, when and if anyone reproaches me and asks why, with my philosophical bent, I didn't marry a novelist, for example. . . . Oh, ladies and gentlemen, I've been so unlucky during my life that so far I've yet to meet even one such appealing person on earth. The sun of education, it seems, should benefit everyone equally, but in fact it turns out that this inner life-giving warmth reaches only very few. . . . The largest part, as, for example, women of the bustle, borrow from the sun only its empty brightness; and the rest, such as women of letters, skimming the surface, get attached to lifeless books and, removed from life, turn into indoor decayed creatures. I don't know why, but at the mention of "women of letters," I always imagine bloodless and shriveled-up girls who, upon waking, bathe in civic tears instead of in fresh water, regard the world through the dark glass of tendentious goggles, and, as they retire for the night, cover themselves with the latest issue of the *News* instead of a sheet, and place a volume of Nadson's[*] posthumous poetry under their heads.

Good thing I missed one like that!

[*]Semyon Nadson (1862–87), a poet whose pessimistic work was characterized by a conflict between despair and dreams of ideal beauty, died at the age of twenty-four from consumption.

Women of the stove—or, to express it in a more elevated way, "women of the hearth"—include, of course, primarily mothers and housewives; this category stands closest of all to real life and therefore is the least demanding. But such is the incorrigible prejudice of an intellectual that he inevitably wants to see a woman with all the cunning tricks of the latest fashionable fad, and he timidly shies away from her once he detects any traces of unspoiled nature and healthy beauty. A woman of the stove . . . our refined imagination immediately conjures up some sort of perpetually ruddy and abusive female in the kitchen, with a common sizzling saucepan in her bare hands, an uncouth creature, lacking both mind and soul, who cleans up the dirt and nurses her child herself. . . .

Ugh, how could anyone want someone like that?

No, it's better to find a woman who wears a fashionable saucepan on her head, who's trying to make a splash, and who doesn't nurse her own child, because her breasts are made of gutta-percha,* the same American gutta-percha from which both her bustle and her heart are formed! And now we encounter the latest evil on earth—*the bustle.* . . . Women of the bustle. . . . Oh, what sort of comparison can there possibly be with women of the stove? What duplicity of mind and pocket are needed to conquer her heart made of gutta-percha? What perfidiously insistent sparks linger in her passionate eyes, innocent and adulterous at one and the same time, and what indescribable charm rings in her resonant, garrulous speech, so elegant and absorbing, so vacant and ambiguous? And most of all—how she can dress, in what impenetrable, defensively flirtatious armor of ribbons and rags she can clothe her frail figure, so that even the incomparable devil can't discern what it's made of originally! A woman of the bustle is not even a woman . . . she's some sort of elusive, subtle combination—of

*A soft, pliable substance made from the latex of a Malaysian tree, used to enhance a woman's bosom.

an inviting smile and lipstick, a bashful blush and pink powder, purity of soul and soft fabric, high heels and striving for the ideal, fashionable perfume and the latest trends. . . . Enchantment, indescribably scrumptious enchantment!

But this crafty inundation is short-lived—it lasts less than half a year, if not merely the length of your honeymoon; then your enchanting other half gradually begins to "show her bustle." From that day begins your sentence of so-called bustle obligation, much more onerous, it goes without saying, than military service, because here you can easily lose your head without ever fighting in a war. While you receive a small salary, live in two rooms facing the courtyard, and have no children, your wife is competing in attractiveness with Savina* and doesn't reveal any visible signs of the coming ordeal. (This is only the first act of the play, the shortest.) On occasion, however, upon return from some sort of absurd *jour fixe,* her face suddenly assumes a languid, suffering expression, and she remarks abruptly to you: "Ah, Jean," or— "Oh, Isidore, someday we'll be as well appointed as the Nenyukovs. I love you very much, but you'll agree, it's simply intolerable to live as we do!" And then, nearsighted Jean or kindhearted Isidore, in order to satisfy his saintly, long-suffering other half, makes the effort, scrounges, behaves like a scoundrel, and finally receives the desired promotion at work.

The second act: your means have increased and you hasten to take up residence in a five-room apartment with a fine main entrance and a doorman. And then the "bustle torture" begins. The first one is Liszt's rhapsody† which your spouse will butcher after dinner on a Schroeder piano purchased quite "by chance." The second torture is your own *jours fixes* at which

*Marya Savina (1854–1915) was a beautiful and famous Russian actress.
†Franz Liszt (1811–86) was a Hungarian virtuoso pianist and composer of the Romantic period. His Hungarian Rhapsodies are among his most popular compositions.

you receive various indistinguishable people who, in gratitude for your hospitality, spread around town all sorts of nasty anecdotes about your married life. And even though during these soporific *jours fixes,* though your bones crack from boredom and from the Liszt's rhapsody with which your wife plagues you, and your wisdom tooth aches terribly, you're relatively satisfied, since your indefatigable other half is apparently content. But, unfortunately, this state doesn't last very long. Your daughter is growing up and your wife justly points out that poor Annette will never get married if you don't organize amateur theatricals for her at home, and that naturally, your apartment is much too cramped to stage such hallowed events—a circumstance that she's hidden from you selflessly during the course of the last ten years (?).

There's nothing to be done; you use the promotion you received after Easter and move to a new location—eight rooms with a large hall for the purpose of staging "mousetrap" performances. Unfortunate man that you are, you don't even suspect that two new, very harsh tortures are being prepared for you: a subscription to the opera and a dacha in Pavlovsk. Without these two adornments, the third act of your marital tragicomedy turns out to be unthinkable and your wife now asserts definitively that in this more proper ambience, you have to live a more appropriate lifestyle, or else you might as well be living in the middle of a slum. Needless to say, you don't want to relocate to a slum, so at one fell swoop you subscribe to the opera and to the Tsarskoye Selo Railway, and from that moment on you begin to conjugate the verb *to live* according to all the rules of "bustle" grammar: in the winter you sleep through symphony concerts, you curse Soloviev's *Cordelia,** you gnash your teeth nervously when, in view of the mousetrapping goal of an amateur performance, your study is transformed into a

Cordelia is the best-known opera by the composer Nikolai Soloviev (1846–1916).

theatrical dressing room, and you're assigned the footman's grimy kennel for your bedroom and study combined; in the summer you run as fast as you can for the train and the horse-drawn tram, and you grow thinner instead of putting on weight because you don't have time to finish your meals, you don't get enough sleep, and you secretly envy the footman's more fortunate dog, Polkan.* But—being a slave of habit—you become reconciled even to this situation, soothing yourself with the happy certainty that finally all of the established bustle torments have been surmounted and that your life, in spite of its twisting and turning, will, at least, not change course anymore. Oh, you numskull, you! You can't even guess that all this is merely the beginning of the end. Now, when you've established yourself comfortably in a more appropriate ambience, both musical and theatrical, both appareled and symphonic, both winter and summer—when, it seems, you should begin to enjoy relatively peaceful days—more and more often your wife begins to manifest symptoms of that fashionable and dangerous ailment that most precisely should be called "bustle-schmerz."† One fine evening, upon leaving with your Marya Dmitrievna or Sofya Petrovna some stupendous spectacle costing you considerable financial outlay, in answer to your question about how she liked the performance, you hear in reply a hollow and painful moan: "It was nothing special!" *Nothing special* (?). This is the ultimate word of bustle-pessimism.

You can overhear this hysterical bustle-wail everywhere the bustle kingdom can be glimpsed—in theaters and clubs, at concerts and *jours fixes,* at suburban rail stations and all sorts of fatal bazaars. Naturally, one must reckon with it. And then the final, most offensive, and ruinous bustle torture begins—the feverish search for that mysterious "special" quality in various

*Polkan was the name of the general in Tsar Dodon's army in the opera *The Golden Cockerel* (1907) by composer Nikolai Rimsky-Korsakov (1844–1908).
†See above, p. 38.

foreign and domestic medical stations, until, at last, it turns up somewhere in the shade of Crimean vineyards or in some impassable Caucasian ravine in the bestial embrace of the last of the Amalat-beks* (fourth act!).

Then the story is repeated that occurred with my own wife this past summer at the spa in the Caucasus: a woman goes completely crazy, she rants and raves, and as a demonstration of her spousal independence, all at once on the summit of some diabolical mountain she loses her good sense, her conscience, and her bustle—that very same bustle-lawmaker, thanks to whose reforms the contemporary husband has turned into an empty and hollow sound, he has become some conforming inclination, an absolute zero of mankind, a dacha ass, a bustle–bête noire, anything you like, only not what he is really supposed to be.

Oh, if you only knew how dreadfully I hate this villainous bustle, this impudently luxurious, flirtatious, whimsically stubborn bustle, not unlike a woman's heart! I don't know, perhaps I regard such things much too pessimistically, but—be that as it may—I can't see it merely as a woman's worthless rag wound on a frame of reed or wire; in my eyes the bustle is the allegorical expression of a woman's shamelessness and vanity; it is the pernicious source of all family revolutions and the hospitable refuge of the bustle-demon, who takes up cozy and permanent residence there. As a matter of fact, if you're a deceived husband—and, consequently, your vision has become sharper—and if you glance more closely at the bustle, you'll notice a minuscule, puny little demon stuck there, with small horns, a restless little tail, and an extremely satisfied look on his face. When no one is near his newest abode, this bustle demon never shows himself, but if he happens to pass a dacha husband, the demon slips out of the folds imperceptibly and,

*The hero of a popular tale of the Caucasus by the romantic writer Alexander Bestuzhev-Marlinsky (1797–1837).

snorting obscenely, makes a nasty, mocking face at the pass-
erby. . . . You don't believe it? Wait—get married—and that
isn't all you'll get to see!

The fifth act—it goes without saying—is a divorce.

✦

My conjugal confession is near an end. . . . If it happens to
be read by some other husband as unfortunate as I am—I'm
sure he'll shed a sympathetic tear over these melancholy
lines. If an irritable lady reads these lines. . . . No, it's better
if she doesn't: it'll merely poison her existence, but it still won't
spare her from the bustle! If—God forbid—my confession falls
into the hands of a contemporary, painfully sensitive young
woman, and distressed by this unsightly exposure of the conjugal pantomime, she makes a naively uncomprehending face,
then I'll say to her in conclusion, to this nice, oppressed innocence, almost the same thing that Hamlet said once upon a
time to the charming Ophelia:

> If you take it into your head to get married, let the bitter,
> deadly truth be your dowry: withdraw from other people
> or marry a fool—intelligent men now understand all too
> well how unhappy you'll make them. Oh, I know how
> you disguise yourself! God gave you one face, but you
> devise another for yourself. You whiten it, use rouge,
> pencil your eyelids and eyebrows, adorn your mouth
> with foreign-made teeth, expand your bosom with gutta-
> percha breasts, and attach those revolting bustles. . . . You
> destroy your husband with "Hungarian" and other sorts of
> domestic rhapsodies and then convince everyone that he
> died from stomach catarrh; you chatter incessantly about
> your sublime love of science and art, yet always wind up
> with some insignificant lover from the pernicious tribe of

dacha gophers; you hang around in filthy clubs, spending half your life in rented quarters, and come home only to give birth; sometimes you even attend lectures on pedagogy and hygiene, meanwhile relegating your own children to live in something like a drainpipe, reserving your best and lightest rooms for the rabble that frequents your *jours fixes*. . . . All of this is absolutely sufficient to drive the sanest man crazy. . . . No, weddings are no longer necessary! What need is there to multiply the number of dacha husbands? Let those who are married keep on living. . . . To hell with them! As for the rest, let them, as best they can, guard themselves from this ignominious bustle captivity. . . .

Enough of this hypocritical interlude presented under the sacred name of "marriage." Enough, enough!

6

A Convention of Dacha Husbands

IT WAS A VERY STRANGE, almost unbelievable "convention."
. . . A small group of insulted and injured* husbands gathered
together, in secret from their wives, in a separate room of a
suburban Petersburg restaurant, for a general discussion of contemporary marital misfortunes and a search for some means to
protect their human rights. It was, so to speak, a small conspiratorial attempt to air publicly for the first time the burning
issue of the "family problem"—an attempt, of course, that if
successful could lead to the expansion of such "marital conventions" and, God knows, perhaps to the subsequent organiza-
tion of an entire network of them in other provincial centers.

Although the aforesaid first meeting had been designated
a "convention of dacha husbands" as a joke, in reality its par-
ticipants were in no mood for joking, and their general appearance conveyed the impression of profound misery and
hopeless humiliation, as if each one was thinking to himself,
Yes, my situation is unbearable . . . it's time to die! The howling
snowstorm outside on that nasty winter evening seemed to
reinforce the prevailing mood as it wailed despondently outside the windows, "Yes, indeed, your situation is unbearable. . .
it's time to die!" In addition, on the large dining room table
around which all these dacha husbands were seated, there was
not one drop of vodka, because, according to their previous

*Compare to the title of a novel by Fyodor Dostoevsky, *The Insulted and the Injured*
(1861).

agreement, in view of the exceptional seriousness of the question under consideration, supper was postponed until later and tea was served without cognac.

There were ten people present at the meeting: two teachers, two civil servants, one prosecutor, one lawyer, one scholar, one writer, one artist, and one architect—all men who were no longer young, with very distinguished positions in society, and extremely unenviable situations in their family lives. By the way, one person at the convention (General A), as if he were appearing at a meeting of the finance commission, was sporting tails and a star, but it was obvious to everyone there that the finance commission was merely a pretext and that he was dressed like that intentionally, to convey greater solemnity to the gathering. All the rest of us were in frock coats and black mourning ties, with the exception of the artist who was showing off in a velvet morning coat and wore no tie at all.

Ivan Grigorevich Brusnichny,* a well-known personage in Petersburg, was unanimously chosen as chairman, that very same Brusnichny who in 1887 was careless enough to lose his own wife on the summit of Bermamut, and who in 1889 had the misfortune of finding her again in the valley of the Merchants' Club. This noteworthy meeting opened with his short but profoundly heartfelt speech. After tea was served, the Tartar footmen were sent out of the room, and at the chairman's signal, all private conversation ceased; Ivan Grigorevich cleared his throat in an imposing manner and, with the look of a man who recognized the gravity of the moment, slowly and sadly rose from the chairman's place. . . .

"Kind sirs and kind mad . . ." he was about to say, but on the last word he choked and, turning aside, spat angrily. In a show of sympathy, several other members of the gathering did the same thing, that is, also turned aside and spat. Then the chair-

---

*From *brusnika* (Rus.), "cowberry" or "red whortleberry."

man cleared his throat again, straightened his tie nervously, and continued in an agitated voice: "At first glance, dear sirs, our present gathering may seem somewhat strange! But that's only at first glance. If you consider official meetings of archaeologists and millers, scientists and doctors, as well as various botanical, hygienic, anthropological conventions, and so on and so forth, then why not grant the de facto existence of a meeting of 'dacha husbands'? As a matter of fact, could the security of some dubious historical rock be more important . . . than that of the foundation of human well-being—the *family*? Could it be, dear sirs, that the controversial fight against the hurdle of cholera could appear more important than the imminent self-sacrificing struggle with contemporary women, that most pernicious of all 'hurdles,' on whom, I am convinced, Herr Dr. Pettenkofer* himself would choke?" (Laughter and applause. Some shouted, "Of course not! Of course not!") "Of course not!" the speaker repeated contentedly, and continued: "Some might naturally object that one should not exhibit the family's defects publicly, and that such 'defects' should remain a 'professional secret' for each husband, just as a patient's illness does for each doctor. . . . Let us agree that it does! But for each and every doctor his patient's illness remains his 'professional secret' only so long as that illness is not *contagious* and doesn't threaten all society. . . . Excuse me, sirs, but can it be that our wives' epidemic-like growth of egoism and frivolousness, their moral depravity and psychopathological fastidiousness should not be considered *contagious* and not present a danger to society? Can it be that we don't observe contagious consequences at every step and don't fear in our souls for the future of our families?" "We do see! We do fear! Damn them!" a muffled grumble of voices could be heard around the room. Ivan Grigorevich shook his head defiantly

*Max Joseph von Pettenkofer (1818–1901), the Bavarian chemist and hygienist, wrote an important treatise on the treatment of and protection from cholera.

and, extending his right arm into space, concluded with inspiration: "And so, dear sirs, in view of the threatening danger, let us close ranks amicably—a danger threatening all of us personally, our children, and the future generation of dacha husbands! Let us close ranks—and pity anyone who opposes us!" And, to the unanimous applause of the entire gathering, he lowered himself heavily into his seat.

There followed a long, melancholy pause, bearing witness to the profound impact produced by the chairman's speech. Ivan Grigorevich squinted modestly and, rubbing his hands together in self-satisfaction, addressed the gathering in an artificially indifferent tone: "Well, gentlemen, I think we can now open the discussion. . . ."

But at that moment a tall, lean man wearing blue eyeglasses suddenly rose from his place (the teacher B) and, in a muddled manner, with some nervous impetuosity, declared: "By no means do I wish to offend the respected chairman of this meeting; however, I propose, gentlemen . . . I propose that before we open the discussion, in a certain sense it would be fitting to recall Lermontov's poem 'Borodino!'"*

"Why 'Borodino'? What for?" puzzled voices resounded.

"Allow me to go on, gentlemen, I didn't finish. . . . I myself want to propose that we recall the following well-known verse: 'Then we began to count / Wounds and comrades.' In a word, it seems to me that having assembled to count our familial wounds together, we should remember our comrades in misfortune who perished before their time in unequal battle. . . . Let us recall, gentlemen, Yakov Ivanovich, who threw himself out of a window after a scene with his wife; Nikolai Ivanovich, who threw himself into the Fontanka River; Peter Ivanovich, who threw himself under a horse-drawn tram; and last of all, Fyodor Fyodorovich, who died recently in a lunatic asylum. . . ."

*A lyric poem (1837) by Lermontov that celebrated the heroism of Russian troops who fought against Napoleon's overwhelming forces at a battle in 1812.

An approving murmur circulated among those present. "I propose, gentlemen, that to honor the memory of these victims of the social temperament . . . that is to say, the female temperament or, more accurately, this contemporary female tyranny . . . I propose that we stand to recognize them!"

Everyone, like a single man, rose and stood for a minute with heads bowed in oppressive silence. But the members of the gathering had hardly resumed their seats when the neighbor of teacher B, namely, teacher C, a plump man with small piggish eyes, turned to the gathering with a new speech of reproach: "While supporting in full my colleague's noble proposal," he began in a mellifluous voice, "the idea of honoring the memory of those fallen, so to speak, on the field of family battle . . . I consider it our obligation to remind this venerable gathering of those husbands *morally* slain, who, deserted by their wives, continue to drag out their pitiful existence today in solitary furnished cells. . . . I'm reminded of our splendid Adam Adamovich, rejected by his spouse last autumn and now living in a *chambre-garni** along Bassein Street, or the former convivial fellow and hospitable host, now become an incurable misanthrope—Kasyan Kasyanovich, living in a furnished room on Liteinyi Prospect, or the complete recluse Alexander Vasilievich, who lives on Stolyarnyi Lane, or . . ." But here the chairman couldn't restrain himself; seizing the bell, he cried almost in a moan: "Bogdan Bogdanovich, have mercy on us! If we try to recount all those abandoned husbands—we'll never finish!"

Bogdan Bogdanovich, frowning with hostility, lowered himself into his armchair, and the chairman rang his bell loudly.

"Gentlemen, I propose we start the discussion."

But the discussion was not destined to begin this time either. The architect D, seated at the end of the table, a blond, young-

*Furnished bedroom (Fr.).

looking man wearing a gold pince-nez, who had all the time been concentrating on something or other in a very serious manner, suddenly jumped up from his seat and declared in a shrill voice: "Will you allow me one more word . . . only one?" And hurriedly removing from the side pocket of his jacket a piece of paper folded into four, before all those present, he unfolded a colored sketch of a building. "I confess that I've never contemplated disturbing the order of things; but the question of deserted husbands introduced by Bogdan Bogdanovich unintentionally prompts me to share with this gathering a confidential idea that I had intended to guard carefully as a secret until the first meeting of the architectural society. . . ."

"What idea? What is it?" curious voices asked.

"It's a completely original proposal, gentlemen!" the architect replied in an agitated manner as he handed his design to the nearest member of the gathering. "It's a proposal to build a furnished shelter for deserted husbands . . . modeled on boardinghouses for widows erected in some foreign countries! The entire building is designed in the Moorish style, there's a flag of mourning on the cupola, and the entrance is decorated in . . ."

"Forgive me," replied the artist in an offended voice to the speaker, attentively deciphering the tiny label under the drawing. "It says here, 'Proposal to build a shelter for homeless pedigreed dogs'!"

The architect blushed and slapped his forehead. . . .

"Oh, what an ass I am . . . I grabbed the wrong one! I apologize; this one really is for dogs. . . . I sketched it for tomorrow's meeting of the Society for the Welfare of Aged Poodles, but I have another design for a building . . . and that one really is for deserted husbands. . . . What a memory I have!" he muttered, stuffing his proposal back into his pocket, and sat down in embarrassment.

The chairman's bell rang out again and once more the invitation to begin the discussion was announced to the preoccupied gathering: "Gentlemen, anyone who wishes to speak . . . I ask you to raise your hand."

Two hands went up simultaneously, each holding notes, obviously outlines of what they planned to say. It was the lawyer N, a bald, good-natured old fellow and the writer K—a pale, nervous man with wandering eyes.

After a few affable demurrals, the lawyer N, as the senior of the two, was recognized. The lawyer's appearance, it turned out, was very deceptive. As soon as he stood and began speaking, his face suddenly grew vicious, his eyes filled with blood, and he bared his teeth. . . . He spoke in a manner not at all corresponding to his venerable age—his voice was unnaturally loud, maliciously abrupt, and vengefully triumphant. . . .

"Gentlemen!" he began. "I permit myself to think that the grim question troubling us at the present time is not merely our own domestic, 'Russ-ssian' question, so to speak: but it is, one might say, a broadly European question! Yes, sir, we suffer from today's female fickleness not only in a personal manner, as Russians; now all lawful men, one might say, to a man, are suffering, both here at home and abroad; it's not for nothing that recently ominous and ironic voices in Europe have begun to be heard louder and louder. . . ."

"You say, voices in Europe?" the general with the star asked, cupping his hand around his ear so that he could hear better.

"Yes, sir, gentlemen, even in Europe . . . not only on the banks of the Neva!* Not only, sir!" The speaker frowned venomously and continued: "I'm talking not only about Hartmann and Schopenhauer,† who some time ago appraised all the pernicious extravagance of contemporary woman; before us now the latest, and, one might say, most modern writers—Friedrich

*The main river in St. Petersburg flowing into the Gulf of Finland.
†Eduard von Hartmann (1842–1906), German metaphysical philosopher; Arthur Schopenhauer (1788–1860), German philosopher who emphasized the role of will as the central factor in understanding.

Nietzsche, Lombroso, Strindberg, Ibsen . . .* all of them—including even Ibsen—amicably point out the impending danger. . . ." The elderly lawyer leaned over his outline, to which excerpts of newspaper articles had been attached, and, almost gasping with indignation, he read the following: "A woman's self-love and her aspiration to turn her husband into an indentured servant obliged to fulfill her every desire and whim, grows not by the day, but by the hour, and has started unintentionally to arouse the serious attention of European writers. . . . Mankind has finally begun to notice where this adoration of women has led him. . . . His former slave has gradually turned into a tyrant and threatens her primary support, that is to say, man, with ruin. Apparel, gala balls, nerves, and whims, all this comes crashing down on the unfortunate head of the contemporary spouse. . . . He is required by his work, by his blood to feed this rapacious spider, the contemporary woman, while he has the strength, while his physical and moral health withstand inordinate demands of every kind. . . . The most definitive of all who have thought and written about this is August Strindberg. . . . In his opinion, the contemporary cultured man has two implacable enemies: the crude physical strength of 'the many,' that is to say, the crowd, and . . . female guile. . . . The proletariat and women—these are the two most pernicious enemies of genuine culture, the two destructive obstacles that one may say . . . one may say. . . ." But, as a result of an excess of indignation, the speaker was unable to continue: he was suddenly overcome with a nervous, suffocating cough forcing him to lower himself helplessly onto his chair.

*Friedrich Nietzsche (1844–1900), the German philosopher who challenged the foundations of Christianity and traditional morality; Cesare Lombroso (1836–1909), the Italian criminologist and founder of the Italian School of Positivist Criminology; August Strindberg (1849–1912), the Swedish playwright; and Henrik Ibsen (1828–1906), the Norwegian playwright and poet.

The writer K took advantage of this unforeseen pause to insert his own two cents. . . . He seemed very distressed and distraught.

"The much respected Nikolai Innokentevich, alas, anticipated my thought!" he declared. "Therefore I won't expatiate once more on the significant movement on the European continent as described by the speaker; for my part, I shall lay before this esteemed gathering one clear-cut question, cleverly raised by one of our best-known commentators two years ago in his article on women's emancipation. . . . Answer me this, gentlemen: since the time that women became liberated—has mankind achieved as much in the cultural sphere as it had during the period that women were still slaves?"

The writer adjusted the gold pince-nez on his nose and looked around at those gathered with a proudly ironic glance. . . . Having noticed, however, a slight smile on the faces of several members, he snorted in semi-offended fashion.

"Oh, it seems that not everyone agrees with me that a woman ought to be a slave? I confess, gentlemen, that's very odd! Why then should we be meeting . . . when it turns out there is no solidarity among us!"

The elderly prosecutor, having recovered from his coughing spell, frowned venomously once again.

"No, what do you mean, we're in complete agreement, it's only that . . . but tell us why . . . on principle you always write journal articles in favor of women's emancipation?"

The writer nervously rumpled his flowing locks: "Ah, my God, what don't I write about on principle in journals? But confidentially, in intimate circles, I always passionately maintain that a woman ought to be a slave and ought not to meddle in a man's affairs!"

"Well, what would it cost you," observed one of the teachers, "do you understand, to use your talent and write a novel on this 'confidential' theme. . . . You could, don't you see, perform such an important service to society, such a service!"

"I could write it, gentlemen, I certainly could . . . if it weren't for my own Olga Nikanorovna!" the flattered writer sighed. "But you know, in my family situation, three-quarters of my life is spent on devil knows what!"

"It's precisely the devil who knows what!" the artist agreed and groaned painfully: "Ah, gentlemen, what a painting I could present to the world . . . if it weren't for my Praskovya Semenovna! And why the devil, you ask, did I, an unattached artist . . . suddenly bind myself hand and foot to some woman? And what exactly is a woman?" The artist suddenly slapped the table bitterly and cried defiantly, "Mr. Chairman, what is a woman? We must conduct a general investigation! Or else we'll be spinning our wheels!"

The uninhibited artist's forceful summons momentarily loosened everyone's tongue, and the discussion became collective, boisterous, and incoherent.

Chairman: Hmm. . . . What is a woman? Regarding the definition of a woman, gentlemen, I agree completely with one Indian philosopher who, in all likelihood, was married, and who stated the following: (1) before marriage a woman is a rose without thorns; (2) one day after her wedding, she's a rose with thorns; (3) after two weeks, she's all thorns with no roses. (Unanimous applause.)

Lawyer N: In my opinion, Maupassant was most successful in avoiding marriage. "I won't get married," he said, "because there's no way I can foresee in advance all the stupid things my wife would force me to do!"

Teacher B: I don't understand, gentlemen, why the committee on statistics doesn't open a special division for the numerical calculation of outstanding incidences of female fastidiousness. Such graphic statistical tables would be a great help in the clarification of the fundamental question!

Teacher C: As far as I'm concerned, I must confess publicly that for the last three years I've been keeping absolutely candid memoirs of all my conjugal adversities; at the present time I already have accumulated twelve hefty volumes. . . . I plan on giving them to Shubinsky to publish in the *Historical Bulletin*[*] as a warning to future generations of men!

General A: Ah! Gentlemen, you won't accomplish anything with statistical tables or denunciatory memoirs [alluding to the writer K]. . . . All the trouble comes from women's emancipation, inflamed "on principle" by certain people. . . . My acquaintance, the writer Avseenko, in his remarkable book *On Women*,[†] very accurately observed that the contemporary generation of women began life, so to speak, "with hereditary dizziness." This was an unusually apt remark! Precisely that, "with hereditary dizziness"! That's why everything in our families now is topsy-turvy!

Architect D: It's even terrible to think, Your Excellency, where such a sad inheritance could lead women!

Lawyer N (smiling enigmatically): Well, it goes without saying, it could lead *there*! Where else, once female morality is on the wane. . . . Flaubert predicted it. . . .

General A: Hmm. In what manner? I don't understand you!

Lawyer N: Here's how, Your Excellency! One day his student Maupassant was walking along a deserted lane and saw the famous novelist leaving one of those, don't you know, one of those *houses*. . . .[‡] Maupassant, as they say, gaped . . . "*Maître*[§]— it's you . . . and suddenly from one of those places!" And, in

---

[*]A literary and historical journal published in St. Petersburg from the late-nineteenth to early-twentieth century.

[†]Vasily Avseenko (1842–1913) was a writer, critic, and journalist whose *Letters About Women* was published in 1888.

[‡]A house of ill repute (i.e., a brothel).

[§]Master (Fr.).

reply, Flaubert shook his head sadly and said full of feeling, "L'avenir est au. . . ."*

But the chairman's deafening bell hastened to interrupt the exceedingly uninhibited speaker . . . and Flaubert's spirit was spared.

"Gentlemen, this discussion is like nothing on earth; we've strayed far from our subject!" cried the chairman. "And the main thing is, none of this helps in any way to solve the problem. . . . If we continue in this manner, we'll constantly be distracted by minor details and never get to the heart of the matter. . . . I propose, gentlemen, that we rely, as much as possible, on scientific grounds and make use of this fortuitous opportunity to turn to an authority, Ferdinand Ivanovich." Here the chairman respectfully nodded in the direction of a stunted, stooped old man with a bristly beard, wearing absolutely enormous goggles, more like a horse's blinders than eyeglasses, who was snoozing in his armchair. "Ferdinand Ivanovich!" The scientific authority came to, surveyed the gathering gloomily, and unhurriedly began to clean his blinders. "We're turning to you, much-esteemed Ferdinand Ivanovich, for your valuable scientific experience. . . . Tell us with full candor, what does science say about the contemporary matrimonial question?"

"Yes, what does science say? That would be very interesting!" people said with some agitation. "We're relying on science! Do you hear, we're relying on it!"

Ferdinand Ivanovich rose slowly from his place, slowly adjusted the glasses on his nose, and slowly and thoughtfully uttered: "I must warn you, dear sirs, that the conclusions of European science are not very reassuring . . . especially as related to the goals of our meeting. Science, if one may express it thus, advises us to wait and to endure!"

*The future is for . . . (Fr.).

A restrained groan spread through the room. Ferdinand Ivanovich shrugged his shoulders serenely, implying his own helplessness before the conclusions of science, and continued: "Science, as something that stands above all parties and classifications, sees only the ordinary, transitory condition of human society in the matrimonial adversities we suffer. Outstanding authorities in the West categorically affirm that until both sexes reach sociological equilibrium, antagonism between the two sexes is inevitable; any attacks on the female half of humanity can be considered useless and ineffective. In a word, until they are granted the same standing, there is no definitive basis for making any distinction in their rights; consequently, my dear sirs, it remains for us only to arm ourselves with forbearance and to hope that science in the last analysis, will level everything for the common good!"

In the face of such a scientific conclusion, all members of the gathering felt disheartened. The general with the star was the first to utter a word.

"Allow me, sir, to ask how we can wait. How can we go on living *until* science answers? Shall we just drop dead, or what?"

"It goes without saying that we must take certain steps!" the architect confirmed.

"Steps! Steps! Even if only palliative!" cried the members of the gathering, who looked questioningly at their chairman. Ivan Grigorevich was genuinely bewildered.

"I agree, gentlemen, that we must take steps, but what steps?"

And, frowning in deep thought, he surveyed the gathering.

At this question, everyone present frowned and felt bewildered in turn, with the exception of one lawyer who giggled somewhat ironically into his fist.

"What could you possibly find so amusing . . . at such a tragic, so to speak, moment?" the general observed, staring at him sternly.

The lawyer dropped his eyes, feeling slightly embarrassed.

"I was unintentionally amused, gentlemen, by one thought . . . what sort of steps could be taken against my Nadezhda Emelyanovna?"

The gentlemen at the gathering exchanged expressive glances with one another and also dropped their eyes—most likely each one of them recalled his own Emelyanovna. The oppressive pause lasted for several minutes, during which all the gentlemen at the gathering pensively smacked their lips; then, all of a sudden, as if by an instinct of self-preservation, they all raised their heads and turned in the direction of the enigmatically silent science represented by Ferdinand Ivanovich.

"Ferdinand Ivanovich!" the chairman said, turning to him again. "All our hope rests with you. . . . In your opinion, what steps can be taken?"

Ferdinand Ivanovich surveyed the gathering with his lackluster glance and, without rising from his place, muttered apathetically: "In my opinion, no steps are necessary! What for . . . when in any case, the end of the world is upon us!"

Everyone's eyes opened wide. . . . From this "authority of science" no one, I must confess, no one could've expected such a pronouncement and the majority decided that Ferdinand Ivanovich simply hadn't had enough sleep the night before.

"Most likely, you're joking, dear Ferdinand Ivanovich?" the chairman observed gingerly. "But we're not in the mood for jokes now . . . the question is of great importance!"

Ferdinand Ivanovich cleared his throat, stood up, and wiping his blinders, uttered in a sympathetic, but authoritative voice: "Far be it from me to joke, God preserve me! On the contrary, it's precisely in view of the indisputable seriousness of the dreadful moment that I'm compelled to reveal to you, at long last, science's latest pronouncement on this subject, and I'm resolved to confess to you, dear sirs, my own total solidarity with the opinion of my respected colleague Professor Brandt that . . ."

"What's that? What opinion?" the speaker was interrupted by agitated cries.

"His opinion is very gloomy and definitive, in spite of its complete scientific documentation," continued Ferdinand Ivanovich, raising his blinders to his learned nose. "In his profoundly penetrating article, 'On the Future of the World,' he maintains the validity of the hypothesis that before the geological and astronomical demise of the planet earth, a, so to speak, physiological end will occur—that is, before the stars will be extinguished, all, so to speak, conjugal hopes will be frustrated, and before the earth will cool down and all the seas will dry up, our women will cool toward us men—irrefutable signs of which are on the rise before our very eyes in horrifying progression. . . . Following from this scientific hypothesis, Professor Brandt, with complete justification relegates us, dacha husbands, to the category of 'archaic life-forms'; he reaches the conclusion that in the final days, all power on earth will pass irretrievably and in unlimited manner to . . . women; then it's not far to the reestablishment, to a certain extent, of the despotic 'Kingdom of Amazons.' . . .* I presume, dear sirs, that the facts—which multiply with every passing year and testify to the enslavement of our sex—leave no one in any doubt. . . . Even our present gathering, if one regards it from a scientific point of view, is nothing more than a significant attempt to halt the advancing misfortune. . . . But, alas, our noble attempt can be considered bitter and futile, because the facts of female despotism are increasing, one can say, not day by day, but hour by hour, as if confirming the latest cruel findings of science at every step. . . . Obviously this is the fateful course of history: my dear sirs, we are completely powerless to stave it off!"†

---

*In Greek mythology, a tribe of female warriors supposed to have lived in Scythia, near the Black Sea.

†The apocalyptic theme is reminiscent of that in Leo Tolstoy's novella of jealous rage and sexual abstinence, *The Kreutzer Sonata* (1889).

And, as if in support of the latest scientific findings, the speaker, completely worn out, lowered himself onto his chair. This recent scientific conclusion, and the bitter gravity of tone in which it was uttered by Ferdinand Ivanovich, produced the most depressing impact on the members of the gathering, and a fateful silence reigned in the room, similar to that when someone's sudden death is announced. . . . Everyone's face suddenly grew pinched, their lips twisted in grief, and the noble heads of these seated men, oppressed by the gloom of the perspective revealed before them, impotently drooped to one side. . . . In addition, as a result of the heavy smoking by most members of the gathering, there now hung in the room such thick smoke that even the strongest heads were spinning willy-nilly, and the members themselves, surrounded by clouds of smoke in the pale glow of the candelabra, seemed like some supernatural, funereal ghosts. . . .

One of the men who was sitting closer to the window, and had probably become nauseous from all this "science" and tobacco, spontaneously opened a small, hinged windowpane. A stream of cool, refreshing wintry air suddenly came rushing into the room. . . . The snowstorm had long since quieted down, the sky was clear, and the bright twinkling of the stars shone gravely through the open window on the members of the gathering, conveying mystical solemnity to the reigning silence. At the sight of these stars and the prospect revealed before them, the minds of the members of the gathering were involuntarily focused on the fateful last days of the earth and the imminent Kingdom of Amazons. The mouths of each and every person murmured noiselessly, "My God! What will happen? What will become of us?" It was a long and tragic pause during which, it seemed, a new inspired declaration about the emancipation of the enslaved half of humanity was about to be pronounced. . . . And most likely it would have been . . .

but all of a sudden, in the midst of this profound and significant silence—all of a sudden the sound of bells of an arriving sleigh was heard beneath the windows. Naturally, there was nothing amiss in the fact that a strange troika might drive out to a restaurant in the suburbs of the capital late in the evening; but what was really reprehensible was the transformation that occurred in the demeanor of the chairman at the first sound of the bells.

He suddenly turned deathly pale, clasped his hands together in despair, and uttered in confusion: "Oh, good Lord, it's all over. It's *them!*"

A dire presentiment momentarily seized everyone present. . . .

"Who is it? Who's 'them'?" agitated questions arose all around.

"Our . . . our . . . wives . . ." Ivan Grigorevich was barely able to mutter and then fell into a state of near unconsciousness. But the ferocious cries of the rebellious members of the gathering quickly summoned him back.

"Traitor!" one roared.

"Renegade!" screamed another.

"Informer! Spy!" shouted a third.

And instead of running for the window or the door, they all rushed in embittered despair, almost swinging their fists, at the chairman (with the exception, however, of Ferdinand Ivanovich, who hunched down even lower into his chair and muttered philosophically under his breath: "The fateful march of history . . . alas, alas, alas!").

The architect D took umbrage more than the rest.

"Be so good as to explain this very minute how you let the cat out of the bag," he shouted shrilly at Brusnichny.

"So help me God, gentlemen, I did nothing of the sort!" The flustered Ivan Grigorevich tried to vindicate himself once and for all. "I simply had a small matrimonial squabble with my wife on account of our tickets for Figner* and told her, 'All this will end soon!'"

"What did she say?"

"She asked, 'What will end soon?'"

"What did you say?"

"I replied, 'Your triumph, Madame!'"

"Nothing more?"

"Word of honor, nothing more! So help me God, gentlemen, I myself don't understand how this could happen!"

"But what's happened? Perhaps nothing's happened yet? Why are you attacking this fellow?" the general in the frock coat asked, standing up for the chairman and putting on a brave face. He smiled and remarked, "Perhaps it's simply some boisterous hussars arriving!"

"Oh, if only it were hussars!" The chairman sighed loudly and suddenly, darting from his place, rushed to the window. The majority followed his lead, astonished at themselves for such delayed action. . . .

"One troika, two, three!" Ivan Grigorevich counted in agitation, glancing at the approaching train, and all of a sudden, as if stung, moaned, "No, gentlemen, it's not hussars . . . it's them. . . . Look, don't you see, in the first troika . . . it's my Marya Dmitrievna and your Anna Timofeevna. . . . There in the second—Nadezhda Emelyanovna and Olga Nikanorovna! And there's Praskovya Semenovna with . . . Oh, Lord, we're done for!"

"We're done for! *Sauve qui peut!*"† the bold architect shrieked shrilly, and without thinking for long, threw himself under the sofa closest to the exit. . . . His example proved to be contagious. The writer who struggled "in principle" for the eman-

*The popular Russian tenor Nikolai Figner (1856–1919).
†Every man for himself, or, let anyone who can save himself do so (Fr.).

cipation of women ducked under the table where he'd been sitting; the general in the frock coat sporting a star fled to the curtained window and hid behind the heavy drapes. . . . The remaining members of the gathering were so astounded by the behavior of their comrades that they stood there gaping, without taking any action, and only Ferdinand Ivanovich, maintaining his position and presence of mind, continued to mutter under his breath, "Kingdom of Amazons . . . the course of history . . . alas, alas, alas!"

As a matter of fact, not two minutes had passed before one could hear in the corridor of the restaurant some sort of belligerent commotion similar to the call of the ancient Amazons at the launch of a military assault and—right in the midst of it—piercingly loud voices demanding to know: "Where are they? Where's that scoundrel Ivan Grigorevich? Where's my rascal Ivan Platonych? Where are they, our barbarians? Let us at them!" The door of the conspiratorial study flew open with a loud bang.

✦

Out of respect for the male half of humanity, I shall omit the indelicate details of the ensuing "great bustle-revolution." I profoundly regret that as a result of the foolish carelessness of a certain Ivan Grigorevich, it may be that the beneficial reform of humanity came to nothing.

Just think, all due to a certain Ivan Grigorevich—all was suddenly lost!

However, I'm wrong; not quite all. . . .

By some incomprehensible twist of fortune, the architect D managed to save not only himself but also his humane proposal for a shelter for the care of deserted husbands. I know for a fact that these days, at an extraordinary and secret session of the society of architects, it will be examined out of turn with the assistance of special expertise offered by members of the gathering who survived the "revolution" without suffering any substantial harm.

"Ai-yai-yai! What have we come to? What *have* we come to!"